Sardines

STORIES

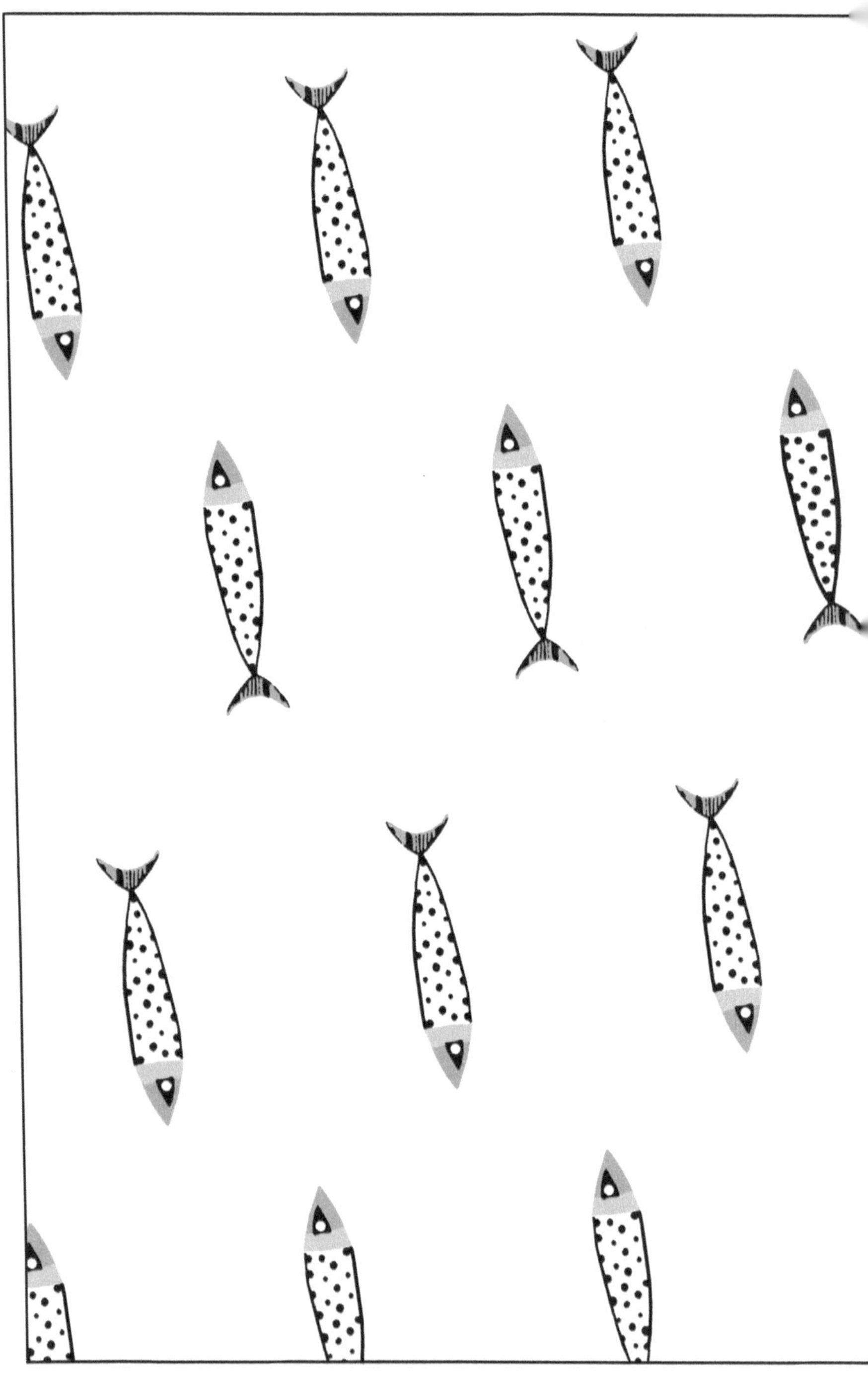

SARDINES

Stories by Angel Dionne

Other Titles by the Author

Mormyridae

Inanimate Objects

Rape Culture 101, as co-editor

ISBN 978-0-9916222-5-2

Published in the United States by ClarionLit

ClarionLit is an imprint of Pen & Anvil Press, a Massachusetts-based publisher founded by members of the Boston Poetry Union and now affiliated with Bonfire Bookshop and Bonfire Press. P&A aims to discover, cultivate, celebrate and promote writing in whatsoever genre, language or mode that is durable, useful, lovely, and relevant. ClarionLit, in coordination with its namesake magazine *Clarion*, is specifically concerned with identifying and uplifting early-career North American authors of exceptional promise. The imprint's colophon device features a turkey, symbolizing New World and the abundance to be found in literature. For all inquiries, the editors can be contacted via *www.penandanvil.com/clarion*.

Layout and design by Zachary Bos.
Text in Minion; titles in VersionType & Beth Ellen

CONTENTS

DEDICATIONS

To my wife, the light guiding me back to myself.

To my mother, the storyteller who helped me find my voice.

To my father, the traveler with a poet's heart.

To David Medalie and the University of Pretoria,
without whom this collection would not have been possible.

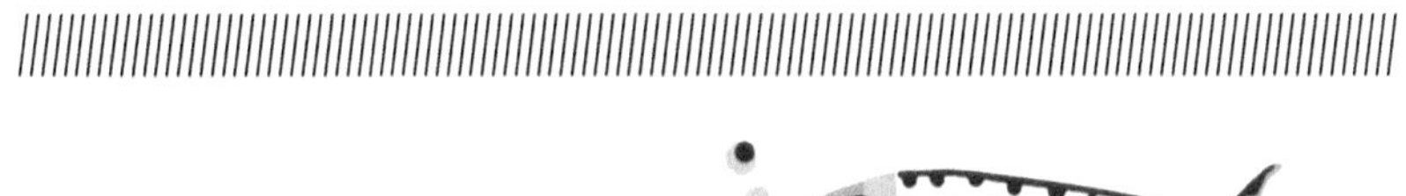

Antoine had always marveled at the way the concrete walls and darkened windows of city buildings were transformed at night. By day, they stood benign, but at night they rose and became towering giants looming high over narrow streets. The tenement buildings and brick storefronts, in crowded desperation, attempted to blot out the moon, and the city sank into a tepid darkness from which Antoine wasn't certain it would ever rise.

Antoine had been born in this city, had grown up in this city, had toiled and agonized and would, as far as he was concerned, die in this city. At sixty-two years of age, he awaited death like one awaits a long-departed lover. He occupied a little ground-floor apartment in a tenement building, facing neither the sunlight by day nor the damp luminescence of moonlight by evening — the perfect place for a forgotten pensioner burdened with arthritis and a stubborn cough.

Although thin-walled, the apartment was good enough to suit him. It wasn't quite home. In fact, the city never really had been despite the fact that he'd never left it. The oppressive air and colourless pavement made up the sum total of his life. Sometimes, he wished things had been different for him.

His retirement, albeit lonely, was comfortable. With his meagre pension, he could afford to rent the only apartment in the building without leaking windows and running water was included in the price. The closet-like sitting room afforded him a place to read the morning paper and although the small window faced a trash-laden alleyway, it suited him just fine. He preferred a view of the alley to one of the sidewalk for fear that, should the window have faced the sidewalk, people would peer through it as they strolled by. After paying the rent, he'd still be left with enough to buy tinned sardines, bread, onions, potatoes, and a few extras. He didn't mind the simple food and in fact preferred it. Although the city often howled of his past failures, he felt the warmth of his good fortune in his bones. The years had been kinder to him than they ought to have been.

While he rarely sought the company of others, for they often talked only of themselves, he'd married once before. The marriage had ended bitterly, and he vowed to never do it again. As far as Antoine was concerned, marriage served no real purpose. Two people living together were bound to hate each other one way or another. Unwashed linen would lead to arguments, and too much whiskey would lead to fist-sized holes in crumbling tenement walls. He had no idea where his wife was now or whether she was alive. The thought of her still being alive somewhere did occur to him quite often. Sometimes, a memory of her wafted over to him — a scent he could not discern, something from another life that seemed to belong to someone else. He could never tell from where it came but only knew that it came from somewhere, and that it briefly brought her back to him. When these thoughts came to him, he shook them off. He'd become accustomed to this life in the same way men like him grow used to stifled lives, to lives spent side-by-side in cramped tenements with barely enough room to breathe a breath without the neighbour hearing it.

Routine had over the years become his closest companion, and he clung to it as though it could keep him from sinking. Every morning, he'd wake at precisely six-thirty, fix a meagre breakfast, and then plop his tired body into his armchair where he'd drink black coffee, eat stale toast, and read the morning paper. It was always bad news, yet the misfortunes of others brought him a sick joy — at least it wasn't him. It struck him as morbid, this ability to find comfort in the afflictions of others. But what could he do? It simply was what it was, after all. He was too old to change himself even if he'd wanted to.

Nothing in the newspaper ever held his attention for too long. His eyes would flit over the obituaries, searching for familiar names. Once he'd finish, he'd sit and watch the hours swim past. Other days, when the sun broke through the city haze, he'd walk.

The only person who bothered to talk with him now was Mrs. Nowak, a hefty, middle-aged woman who lived three streets away in a better part of the neighbourhood. There was a candy store across the street from her apartment, and there was also a café further down, where men on their breaks congregated for coffee and over-priced sandwiches. Mrs. Nowak inhabited a first-floor apartment with her husband and, until just recently, a daughter. They often sat and talked of the past.

She and her husband had arrived from Poland with only a suitcase and dreams of a better future between them. She had been heavily pregnant at the time and due to give birth at any moment. According to her, they'd lived in a closet-like space in her husband's cousin's apartment for the first year after their daughter was born. Three years later, her husband purchased a failed delicatessen and made it into a profitable success. Antoine always listened to her stories although he had no interest in her husband and no interest in things he couldn't afford.

He wondered why Mrs. Nowak bothered with him at all. He'd taken a peculiar liking to her although he'd never admit it. Every time he went on one of his walks, he saw her sitting on the front stoop of her building, watching traffic, and eating a sandwich. Even in the winter, when everyone else hid themselves from the cold the way one hides himself from God, there she sat bundled in a heavy coat and scarf, her mittened hands holding tiny fish nestled between two slices of crusty bread, the oil glistening on her lips and chin.

Loneliness suited Antoine. He had no use for other people, and people had over the years found him useless as well. That is until one snowy midnight in December when he awoke to the sound of someone tapping on the sitting room window. The city was asleep. It was a delicate sound, and he wasn't sure if he had even heard it. He stood slowly, bony frame draped in a thin sheet, and peered into the sitting room. There he saw the darkened silhouette of a cat poised on the windowsill. It looked like shadow painted against a wintry backdrop. He whistled a little sigh from the corner of his mouth and slapped the window as hard as he could. The cat fled. Antoine shook off the bizarreness of the whole situation, climbed back into bed, and fell asleep.

He woke to a city teeming with noise. Life had continued around him as he slept. He rubbed his face vigorously to get his blood flowing. Then, he got up to make breakfast. He had just started buttering a piece of bread when he once again heard the softy tippity-tap of tiny nails against glass. The cat had returned or had otherwise spent the night skulking about the outside of his home. He wasn't sure what to do, but he did know that he didn't particularly care for the cat's presence. He laughed to himself when saw it again — a brown tiger-striped cat with a notch at the tip of its right ear. Every few seconds, the skinny animal gave out a pleading mewl. Antoine pressed his lips, trying to fight off a horrible feeling he could not identify. The cat's persistence annoyed him. He cared less for animals than he did for people.

Resolving to ignore the cat, he sat and read his paper as usual. Thirty minutes passed. Then, an hour went by. Still, the cat remained a statue placed upon his windowsill. Exasperated, he marched his thinning bones to the bedroom, where he shut the door against the cat's desperate sounds.

When he no longer heard the cat's supplications and felt satisfied that it had departed, he opened the door and stepped out into the sitting room. As soon as the cat became aware of his presence, it continued its whining sounds. In a fit of rage, Antoine took his shoe from beside the from door and, entering the sitting room, heaved it at the window. It bounced off the glass and landed on the floor with a thud. The cat, startled by Antoine's display of anger, gave out one final trill before retreating to the snow-paved city streets. Antoine looked out the window at its tracks and then went back to his day.

By noon, the sky had brightened, and the snow had subsided to a gentle flurry — the entire city a shaken snow-globe. Desperate for some fresh air, he pulled on his warm winter coat and ventured out into the street. An alabaster sky greeted him from behind a layer of cottony clouds. The sun, like mother-of-pearl, gave off a faint whiteness that provided no warmth. Antoine meandered mindlessly past the ashen titans that lined both sides of the street. Every so often, a window would open, and someone would yell or spit or hack. Small groups of older children congregated in alleyways to talk amongst themselves in hushed tones, feathered white breath floating up from their lips. Antoine watched it with a detached boredom. Each day was indistinguishable from the last, and he wondered whether that was the same for everyone else. It wasn't until he saw Mrs. Nowak's rounded belly and thick, greying hair that he perked up a bit.

"Mr. Levinson," she called out. "Cold day, isn't it?"

She waved a fat arm high above her head.

"Hello, Mrs. Nowak. Cold indeed."

He studied her carefully. She was quite a bit younger than he was, but she gave off the air of a woman well past her youth.

"No sandwich today?"

"I'm afraid not. You must have heard by not what happened to my Ben? He fell sick last week, and we've closed the ship since then. I don't have a head for these things. Besides, who would keep things up at home if I kept the shop open? Oh, it would be a disaster. The doctor doesn't know for how long he'll be sick, so we keep careful about our food for now."

"I hope Ben feels better soon."

"This is the first you hear of it?"

Antoine clenched his jaw. How else and where else would he have heard of it? He shook his head and tried to put on a concerned face.

"Pfft," she said, sucking her teeth. "Every day, it's the same. But when something interesting happens, it's at our expense. You know Sophie rarely visits now. She never bothers to come see her old father and mother — never even bothers to take a break from her studies to lend a hand in the shop while her father, her poor father who gave her everything, rests sick in bed. All this, Mr. Levinson, all this it's too much for my heart. Did I tell you I have a bad heart? All the curse is upon us and what did we ever do but work hard and pray?"

"I'm sure it'll end up alright in the end, Mrs. Nowak. Things usually do."

He cringed at the lukewarm platitude but couldn't think of anything else to say. She seemed to brighten up; her stiff face softened. Figuring that they had nothing left to say to one another, Antoine tipped his hat, wished her a good day, and continued his walk.

He thought about the cat. He didn't want to think about it; he hated to do so, but he couldn't help it. He wondered whether it had found another window to occupy or whether it still lolled about his, hoping for a scrap of kindness. For the first time in a long while, Antoine felt sad for something other than himself.

The sun had already darkened by late afternoon. Light, crystalline talc settled on the hoods of cars and the hats of men. Famished, Antoine collected a few tins of sardines from the grocery on his way home, but once he'd arrived and had taken off his hat and coat, he was disappointed to find that his hunger had left him. The thought caused his stomach to sour. And so, craving neither food nor sleep, he settled down to re-read the paper. He'd often read it more than once, each time pausing to consider the multitude of lives that existed outside of and independent of his own. A group of students in Madrid had been parading in the streets for something or other. The Germans now occupied Poland and were continuing south. Tired of reading, he folded the paper on his lap and thought of the conversation he'd had with Mrs. Nowak. He thought of her daughter Sophie, whom he'd only seen a handful of times. He remembered her, seventeen, sitting on the stoop by her mother's side. He remembered her dress, short and above the knee, and his old heart quickened as his memory traced the soft blush of her youthful cheeks and the shape of her growing breasts. He shook his head, half disgusted with himself, and yawned into his hand. It was still early, but he felt tired enough to go to sleep, and he dropped into a dreamless slumber the moment he climbed into bed.

Another four inches of snow had fallen overnight. The cat had visited again as evidenced by the snowy impressions outside the window. Antoine couldn't understand why this bothered him and why the pawprints in fresh snow suffused him with such dread. His shoulders felt heavier than usual. Everything ached. He knew that it was going to be a difficult day when he realized that he was still without hunger, but nevertheless he peeled open a can of sardines and choked down his morning coffee. He ate mindlessly, barely pausing to chew between mouthfuls of oily fish.

His painstaking meal was interrupted when the cat jumped back up onto the windowsill and sang hoarsely. Antoine could hear it from the kitchen, rebuking him. Was the animal perhaps sick? All he needed now was a sick animal loitering around his home. He considered throwing another shoe, slapping the window again, but the louder the animals lamentations became, the worse Antoine felt. The woeful cries rushed through him until he could neither ignore them nor act in anger against them. Instead, he forked two sardines into a paper bag and brought them to the window. The cat danced a bit on its frozen feet when it saw him approaching with an oil-soaked bag in hand. Antoine pulled the window open and placed the bag onto the snow. The cat ate ravenously and had soon finished the small meal before looking up at him with sad, sea-glass eyes demanding more. Fearing that he'd already encouraged it enough, Antoine closed the window. He watched as the cat hesitated and then jumped down from the windowsill, fading into the frigid mist of a polar December morning.

Later that day, it occurred to him that he must speak with Mrs. Nowak. He needed to share the story of the cat's visits with her. The walk to her street was quicker than usual. His shoulders had lightened and his legs, although still stiff, no longer ached. Mrs. Nowak was sitting in her usual spot on the shoveled stoop. She saw him approach and smiled at him through a mouthful of food. The smell of onions hung in the air around her.

"Good day," she said, swallowing down a morsel of food.

"Good day to you too. How are you?"

"You'll never guess it, but Ben woke up like new. The doctor says it's a miracle because he'd said it would be at least a few weeks that Ben would have to be in bed. Then, just like that, brand new!"

She took another bite and chewed quickly, smacking her lips.

"Give Ben my blessings. Say, something interesting happened to me as well. Something very bizarre, actually. There's a cat that's been hanging around my window. At first, I didn't think much of it, but it's been coming every day now and looks hungry."

"Filthy animals, cats. Be careful about fleas. My neighbour, her heart is too soft for hungry cats, and now she has fleas that bite her legs and live in her clothes and hair. She can't be rid of them. I told her to get rid of the cats, but what does she listen? Nobody listens to me anymore."

"I won't let the cat inside."

"Careful not to be bit either. Filthy animals."

"I think it might belong to somebody. It seems friendly enough."

"Filthy, dirty animals," she repeated. "Best to scare it off with a broom and hope it doesn't come back."

"I'll consider that. In the meantime, maybe I could make up some flyers to see if the cat belongs to someone. It might be missing."

She tsked under her breath and returned to her sandwich. Taking this as an indication that the conversation had run its course, Antoine turned towards home.

He didn't have to wait long for the cat to return. When the sun had set into yet another wintry night, the familiar tip-tip-tap announced the cat's arrival. Antoine shot up from his chair, hoping the cat wouldn't run away before he'd had the chance to feed it. Rushing to the kitchen, he emptied an entire tin of oily sardines onto a plate. He presented them to the cat who ate greedily and then proceeded to look up at Antoine as if to protest the cold.

"It's not me who chooses the weather," he said. "Not much I can do about it, is there?"

The cat quickly weaved past Antoine and into the apartment where it jumped onto the armchair and made itself comfortable, curling up into a tight ball. Antoine's first thought was to grab the ragged animal by the scruff of the neck and throw it into the nearest snowbank. But, as the cat curled its crooked tail over its nose, Antoine felt he'd better leave it. He shut the window tightly and looked at the cat one more time before he turned off the light. The next morning, he found the cat had remained in much the same position. He tip-toed about the apartment so as not to disturb it from its sleep. It wasn't until he'd poured the morning coffee that the cat stirred from its rest and came sauntering around the corner.

Antoine reached down and patted its head then smiled when the cat pressed its wet nose firmly into the palm of his hand.

"It isn't mine," he reminded himself.

He reached for a pad of paper and a pen and scribbled a brief description of the cat: *Found cat — Tiger-striped with green eyes and a notch on the right ear. Friendly. If missing, please call.* But he didn't own a telephone. He thought for a moment and realized that he could ask Mrs. Nowak to list her number.

He folded the paper into his pants pocket and gave the cat another scratch beneath the chin. Before he left, he opened the window a crack and the cat, eager to return to its life, bounded past him and out into the snow-blurred city.

Antoine didn't mind walking through the snow. It had been snowing for much of the week. It was the type of weather that brings with it a weighty silence — one that absorbs all sound and all suggestion of life.

Mrs. Nowak's stoop sat unoccupied, seemingly desolate without her heavy body roosting upon it. He ascended her steps and rapped the front door with his knuckles. No answer. He knocked again. When there was still no answer, he knocked a final time and soon heard clunky footsteps drawing closer. Mrs. Nowak opened the door and stood there in her white nightdress, her face the colour of rotting fruit.

"Sorry to bother you. I saw that you weren't outside, and I needed to ask whether you have a telephone. I'd like to list your number on my flyer."

She arched her eyebrows and pressed her lips into a thin line.

"Would you mind? I don't have a telephone. It's for the cat that I told you about yesterday. Maybe if you get a call, you can tell me the next time I see you."

She plucked the paper from his hand and wordlessly closed the door. Antoine waited. Then she opened the door and handed the paper back over to him.

“I wrote the number there down at the bottom,” she said, pointing.

Her voice was dull, flat. He thanked her and then tacked the flyer to a corkboard outside the grocery. It was all he could think to do.

The cat appeared at its regular time. As he'd done the night before, Antoine opened the window and allowed the cat to settle into the warmth of his chair. That night, he slept fitfully. A series of complicated dreams broke up his normally effortless sleep — contorted faces pasted grotesquely against windowpanes, hands and gnarled fingers reaching out from the walls and tearing at his flesh until nothing was left of him but cracked bones and a mass of pulpy meat. He languished painfully in the limbo between consciousness and slumber. Then, with the first hints of sunlight glowing steadily against the winter pallor, he sat up and coughed wetly into his hands. His chest was heavy, his head filled with bundles of sopping wet cotton. Another cough broke loose a wad of greenish mucus which he spat out into a tissue. Unwilling to rise from bed, he remained still. The room titled whenever he opened his eyes. It wasn't long before the cat popped its pointed ears over the top of his bed.

Sensing that something was amiss, it leapt onto the end of the bed, chirped loudly, and settled at Antoine's feet where it remained for the rest of the day, keeping watch.

At dusk, Antoine finally found the strength to sit up when he realized that it was Friday. He'd stopped praying years ago and had long ago abandoned faith. He'd replaced his faith with a staunch belief in the meaninglessness of things and the relentless nature of time. This Friday felt different. Something called to him and despite the stones in his chest, he rose to light the candles he'd kept tucked away in the pantry. He chanted what little he remembered of the blessings. It was the best he could do with what little he had. His fatigue threatened to press him flat against the kitchen floor and so he returned to the bed and drifted into a hot, sticky sleep where he once again dreamed of monstruous visages from somewhere deep within the fluid density of a high fever. The cat, unperturbed, remained snoring at his feet.

The smell of smoke is what first woke him and then, the sound of something crackling. He bolted upright, his stomach heaving in his throat, and was horrified to find that smoke billowed from the kitchen entrance. It filled the entire apartment with thick, dusty plumes. He ran as fast as he could and filled a pot with water. The candles had been knocked over in the night and had set flame to his checkered tablecloth, and it took two pots of water to extinguish the fire. The tablecloth had been ruined. The apartment smelled of burnt fabric and smoke, and the fire had eaten away at parts of the wooden table while mercifully leaving other parts of it untouched. The cat, bothered by the commotion, sat in the corner of the kitchen licking at a spot on its left leg that had been burnt clean of fur. A reddened wound blistered angrily up to the cat's shoulder, and the cat licked vigorously, attempting to sooth the pain. Antoine saw little charcoal prints leading from the fallen candlesticks to the floor and felt an unholy anger.

He admonished himself for not having heeded Mrs. Nowak's warnings. Grabbing the broom from the pantry, he swatted at the wounded animal until, still hunched over in pain, it screamed and limped from the safety of its corner to the sitting room window. There, he grabbed the cat roughly by the neck and heaved it out into the snow. Looking once more at the frightened, bleeding animal, he slammed the window shut and fell into his chair. Everything burned — his chest, his throat, his eyes. The cat climbed back onto the windowsill and cried hoarsely. Antoine listened to its mournful wailing until his mind, no longer able to tolerate it, took rest.

Piece by piece, hour by hour, Antoine felt his body deteriorating, dismantled like an old automobile being stripped for parts. He remained in bed for much of the morning, choked on his breath, and wished to die. A sickening presence had rooted itself in his belly. Around noon, he managed to rise, fever-wracked, and looked woefully at the rid-tinged snow outside his window. He couldn't stay in the apartment any longer with its claustrophobic walls that smelled of smoke. He couldn't bear to look at the drops of blood in the snow.

It took him twice as long as usual to reach Mrs. Nowak's stoop. Everything around him passed in a dizzying haze — cars, pedestrians, children pushing past on their way somewhere — everyone in a hurry. The city circled him — a carousel of littered streets and distant sirens.

"Mr. Levinson!"

Antoine didn't recognize the voice at first. Mrs. Nowak trotted towards him on the ice. She held a small strip of paper in her hand.

"You don't look so well," she said as she studied his shrunken shoulders and glassy eyes. "You look like my Ben before he took sick. Did I tell you? Ben took sick again. As soon as he gets well, he goes back to be sick. It's just my luck. Lousy, lousy luck. You better get yourself to a doctor, Mr. Levinson. Better now than later."

He opened his mouth to say something but made no sound. His jaw hung limp, his throat dry.

"I got a call for you this morning. A woman says she lost a cat a few weeks ago. It fits what you wrote on your flyer. She gave me this number and says you should call to speak with her. You can come in and make that call now if you'd like."

Antoine waved her away, batting at the air as though to swatting mosquitos.

"You really should get yourself looked at," she yelled to Antoine as he turned away.

For the next two days, he opened cans of sardines with trembling hands and set them in the snow outside his window. They remained uneaten, collecting snow. His health grew poorer by the day, but he was nonetheless hopeful — hopeful that the cat would return, its leg scabbed over, its bruised body healing. But every day, he was greeted by an empty windowsill and a sharp disappointment that lingered in his chest. His breathing had become strained. After another three days, when he realized that the cat hadn't and perhaps would never return, he opened the window and sat in his chair and wished for death.

With its unpredictable and ruthless winds, winter brought with it that night one of the heaviest frosts of the season. The cat, sensing the cold, limped its damaged body into the alleyway where it sniffed at the snow-laden sardines and carefully — because it had not forgotten the broom — poked its head into the apartment. The prospect of warmth drew it indoors, where it jumped up onto Antoine's lap before quickly jumping back down. Antoine's thighs and belly had grown cold. His chest was motionless. The cat retreated further into the apartment seeking warmth and a safe place to lick its festering wounds. On the sitting room floor, snow from the open window collected around Antoine's bare feet.

It wasn't until a week had passed that Mrs. Nowak grew concerned about Mr. Levinson's absence. The last time she'd seen him, she'd been struck with the impression of a gaunt specter drifting across ice and snow — the image of someone already dead. Although Ben warned her not to interfere in matters that weren't hers to interfere in, she looked up Antoine's address and decided to visit him if only to give herself peace of mind.

Mrs. Nowak neared Antoine's apartment and was taken aback by the look of things, by the ominous and unworthy tenement buildings with their decaying facades, with the dumpsters that sat overflowing with trash and a powerful stench, with the laundry lines on which stained undergarments and ripped pants were suspended like time-worn flags. She pinched her nose and knocked on Antoine's door. After several failed attempts, she walked to the corner of the building and down the alleyway where she found the sitting-room window. Her stocking legs sunk into the snow, but she trudged forward, concerned that the window had remained open in such cold. She was too short to see over the window, and so she hoisted herself up on her elbows, her feet dangling against the brick building.

Antoine sat in his chair, his body blue and bloated. Coiled on his frigid lap was the cat. Mrs. Nowak screamed a series of guttural noises and fell from her elbows down onto the ice, her ankle snapping beneath her weight.

The cat jumped up onto the windowsill, its leg still swollen and weeping. Passers-by could hear nothing that morning but the distant incantations of a wounded animal.

a Rainy Day

Miriam's eyes traced the crooked, aimless path of a single raindrop. The rain had begun to seep through the cracks around the window's edge, trickling downward and leaving a wet trail that puddled on the linoleum floor. She looked at it, solemnly, her mind filled with incomprehensible static. It had been raining for precisely two days and one hour. She'd kept track of the weather using the wooden clock above the gas stove. She hated that clock. Her husband had gifted it to her during their first year of marriage and, at first, she'd liked it. It was hand-carved and painted a rich mahogany hue. Vines had been etched around the border. She'd loved nature and had, as a girl, dreamed of someday living in a house with creeping vines that snaked their way from garden to roof, the home consumed by vegetation. Perhaps that's why her husband had chosen the clock hoping that it might bring her a piece of the nature she longed for in their city apartment. Over the years, he'd gifted her with a fern — which now sat wilted in the far-right corner of the bedroom — and a preserved butterfly pressed between two pieces of glass. She hadn't had the heart to tell him that these things only made her resentment deeper. She felt she'd left herself behind when they moved into the city shortly after marriage. She saw in her mind's eye the covered porch where they'd have coffee at sunrise, the apple trees in the back, the twisting vines and the white clover that would entice bees. Their apartment was comfortable, but she felt it would eventually become her tomb.

These days, she studied that clock. She'd been studying it for two days and one hour; two days and one hour of stale air. Two days and one hour stuck in her apartment, unable to see the sky hidden behind dense clouds. She only found herself able to sleep when the beating roar of rain found a temporary lull. Otherwise, the pitter-patter-pat, whistling wind, and occasional bursts of thunder kept her awake.

Miriam gathered her blanket around her shoulders and held it tight across her chest. She watered the wilting fern, hid the dead butterfly in her bedside drawer, and returned to the kitchen to watch the clock. The rain chattered to her in an incomprehensible tongue — a harsh language. She had felt herself called to a self-imposed state of solitude since her husband's death. She hadn't realized she'd fallen asleep at the table until the doorbell rang that somber Tuesday at exactly nine o'clock in the morning. She paused to make certain that she wasn't hearing things. It could happen sometimes. The mind often makes noise out of solitude. But then it rang a second time, and then a third time. The fourth ring was desperate enough to raise her from beneath her stone of thought. She cast the blanket from her body like a shell that had become too small.

"Hello?"

She called out from the kitchen's edge as though frightened by the possible response.

"Yes, hello!"

"What do you want?"

"Miriam?" asked the strange voice. "Miriam Smolinsky?"

She rocked on her heels at the sound of her name. It didn't sound like it belonged to her spoken in that thick, funny voice. For a brief moment, she questioned whether she really was Miriam Smolinsky. Maybe she was somebody else now, had become somebody else without noticing it. At least, she hoped so. Yes, Miriam Smolinsky had been consigned to the past, a past where her husband was still alive and where they lived in a quiet, rural area with apple trees and sun-warmed patios.

The voice did not sound familiar, so she remained there, unable to open the door. Certainly, she'd have remembered such a voice — a voice of rusted tin.

"Who wants to know?" she finally asked.

"An old friend."

"I don't recognize the voice. You have the wrong Miriam."

"I trust you don't remember, Mrs. Smolinsky. I trust you don't. I'm here on official business. Could you please open the door so that we can speak face-to-face?"

"No."

"Why not?"

"Because I can't think of any reason why I should."

"I trust you don't. I trust you don't. But, if you could just do me the favor of opening the door, Mrs. Smolinsky. Open the door, and I'll let you in on the reasons I'm here. You let me in, and I let you in — that's the bargain I'm willing to make. I swear to you on my mother's grave; I'll let you in on the reason I'm here."

She recoiled at the rhythm of his voice and the funny cadence with which he spoke, his voice rising and falling with each word as though some words were too heavy and others too light.

"How do I know you don't mean me any harm? I don't make a habit of opening doors for strangers."

"It's a terrible, rainy day, Mrs. Smolinsky. Some rainy past two days, to be exact. Now why would I, if I were a common criminal or a debt collector, walk all the way here in my good shoes only to take advantage of a recently widowed young woman? A widow who, likely, doesn't have much to her name. No, I don't mean you any harm. So, if you'd just open the door, Mrs. Smolinsky, we can continue with our business."

What could this man possibly want if not to rob her, steal something from her, or strip her of something important? The fact that he knew her name and knew of her husband's death worried her. She thought about his reasoning. A criminal wouldn't announce himself at the door like a salesman. Even a debt-collector wouldn't be out in such dreary weather. Her husband had known many people, but she did not. She could count on one hand the men she knew — her father, her brother with whom she hadn't spoken in months, and of course her husband if she could still count him.

"I can hear you breathing, Mrs. Smolinsky. Do me some kindness and open the door. My feet ache, and my shoes are soaked through. I could use a bit of tea with lemon or something to eat. I've come a long way to speak with you. We can have a chat soon as you open the door, and we'll discuss my reasons for being a nuisance in such weather and so early in the morning, too. I do apologize, Mrs. Smolinsky. I do. But, you see, I didn't have much choice in the matter. You must think me a scoundrel or a pest, but I swear to you on my mother's grave that I mean no harm. There's no ill will — just a friend talking to another friend."

She stepped forward and poised her hand upon the doorknob, then quickly pulled it back.

"Say what you need from behind the door. There's no reason that I should let you in. I can hear you just fine from in here."

"This is a delicate matter, Mrs. Smolinsky. Delicate and private indeed. It would be best to discuss it inside otherwise, the neighbours will hear; you wouldn't like that very much. A good woman doesn't air her dirty laundry for all to see."

She'd lived a simple and unassuming life, and so she couldn't think of anything that would be private enough or scandalous enough to hide from the neighbours. She did, however, worry that the neighbours might hear this strange man and his odd voice echoing through the corridors. A sudden stillness enveloped her. The rain had ceased its noise, and this lull struck her as some sort of sign — an otherworldly quiet. She turned the knob, pulled the door slightly ajar, and found herself greeted by an odd little man drenched in shadow and rain. The bare bulb in the corridor had burnt out, and only a thin trickle of light from the window at the far end of the corridor rested upon on. She could feel the darkness, palpable, sour, and curdling on her tongue. The man's head reached no higher than her chin. His angular cheekbones, casting their shadows, gave him the look of a starved man, while his protruding belly pressed against a shrunken wool coat. He was bald save for two thin, wispy clumps of brown hair on either side of his head. His long, knotted beard dangled against his chest and, as he had said, he had on a pair of good leather shoes.

"Thank you, Mrs. Smolinsky. Thank you. I trust your morning is going well despite my unexpected intrusion," he said, wiping the corners of his mouth. "Would you be kind enough to show me inside so that I can sit? You see, I've been walking for nearly two hours to find you. I misplaced your address, I'm afraid. My legs aren't what they used to be. Like most things, they tire with age and if I don't sit soon and get something to eat, I'll die right here in front of your door. God forbid. God forbid."

"I don't have much to offer for food."

"No need; no need. I'll eat anything you have to give, and I won't eat much of it at all. Despite what it might look like, I don't have a big appetite. Even just a piece of dry bread will do."

He rubbed his hands over his swollen belly and licked his lips.

She ushered him into her home and led him to the kitchen, where he clumsily dropped his square frame into a chair. Then, she reached into the icebox and retrieved half a block of cheese along with a loaf of bread. She sliced the bread, careful to avoid the blue spots dappling the crust. After she'd carefully arranged the cheese and bread on a plate, she brought it to the table. She sat opposite this queer little man who had yet to tell her his name. He reached over, took a slice of cheese with his red fingers, and brought it to his lips."

"Have some bread," she offered, suddenly feeling a sense of pity for the man.

She'd been taught to be kind to company, and she'd always enjoyed it when her husband brought friends and students over for meals. They'd never been well-off, but they'd always made it a point to keep something in the house for guests. Ignoring her, the man reached over and took another piece of cheese.

Miriam shifted uncomfortably as he ate. Bits of half-masticated cheese squelched between his tongue and yellowed teeth. It was all she could hear. He chewed with his mouth open and even the rain, which had again picked up, failed to diminish the sound. A milky residue collected at the corners of his mouth with each bite. Miriam had to look away, and so she studied her thumbs and picked at her cuticles — a habit her husband had hated.

When he'd finished off the cheese, he sniffed his fingers and slumped his misshapen body forward, resting his chin on his hands.

"You must wonder why I come here today to see you? Who is this man? You ask yourself since I rang your bell. You see, I know you. Old friends in spirit, I have to confess. I knew your husband, Mrs. Smolinsky. I knew him well. God rest his soul."

She thought back to the people her husband had brought home — students, colleagues from the school, cousins. She didn't often speak to her husband's guests, but she knew she'd never seen this man before. She knew beyond any possible doubt that this man sitting at her table and eating her food was a stranger. Could he possibly have known her husband? Yes, it was possible. The man's face grew heavier by the minute, and she wondered whether her husband had kept secrets, had hidden away a part of his life.

"You know my husband," she repeated. "You studied with him, then? You teach at the school?"

"I'm a scholar. A scholar of philosophy, to be exact."

The man eyed the bread but hesitate to reach for it. He shook his head as though casting off an empty shell of thought.

"We worked together a long time, your husband and me."

"It's curious, then, that he never had you over. I'm certain I've never seen you before."

He stared at her, his left eye bulging further than the right.

"We were quite close at work, I assure you, Mrs. Smolinsky. Before he took ill and died, we'd have coffee in his office regularly. God rest his soul. Your husband, he never mentioned my name?"

"I don't know your name."

"It's Ed; Edward to some, but Ed to your husband."

"He never mentioned you."

"Be that as it may, the reason I never come over before when your husband was alive, Mrs. Smolinsky, is because I'm not much one for company at all. Your husband, he understood this. An understanding man, he was."

"We never hid things from one another. I'm sure he would have mentioned you if you were as close as you say."

He clucked his tongue and looked at her pitifully. Pity was something she didn't need.

"I can't say I'm surprised. I can't say I'm surprised at all. But the fact of the matter is, we knew each other. This is undeniable, Mrs. Smolinsky. It's as undeniable as this rain that's been falling around us for two days. It's as undeniable as the fact that I'm here in your kitchen. Whether he mentioned me or not, I exist. Would you at all doubt my existence, Mrs. Smolinsky? I exist, and you exist, and we are here right now existing together."

She looked at him. His words shook something loose inside of her, and she decided to change tack.

"Ah," he explained, holding a hand up as if ready to strike her. "Yes, I remember now. I did indeed visit here once. You were asleep then if I remember. I only stopped by briefly to lend your husband a book."

"Which book?"

"*Between Man and Man*."

"Buber," she said.

He nodded. She'd indeed seen this book sitting on her husband's shelf in the bedroom. She'd leafed through it on occasion but had found its contents much too dry for her tastes.

"You must, at least, have some belief in what I say now, Mrs. Smolinsky. Even the faintest of beliefs, no?"

Although she could recall neither his name nor the sound of his voice, she nodded. She tried to concentrate on the sound of the rain if only to escape the dreadful noise that the man's tongue made against the sides of his cheeks whenever the conversation idled.

"So, we've never spoken, Mrs. Smolinsky, but I do know you. Many times, your husband told me of you. He even showed me your photograph. He told me that you never had children. It's an awful thing to say, but I'm thinking I know you now as well as he did. I apologize ahead of time if what I say is too direct. The last thing I want is for me to make you uncomfortable. My mother if she were alive today, wouldn't stand for such things. Never make a lady uncomfortable in your presence, she taught me. A wise person, my mother. May I call you Miriam now? Mrs. Smolinsky seems to me now too impersonal for such a personal conversation. Don't you think so, Miriam?"

She listened to him the way people listen to bad news. The more he spoke, the more unfamiliar he became. *Between Man and Man* was a lucky guess. What teacher of philosophy wouldn't have such a book? Since the beginning of their marriage, he'd piled books wherever there was room — the living room table and floor, the bedside tables, the large bookshelf in his office that collected paperbacks and hardcovers and papers on a myriad of topics. He'd been tormented by an insatiable thirst for knowledge. His topics of interest would shift every few months, and Miriam always came away from their conversations feeling as though she'd learned something new, something of weighty importance. This man was so unlike her husband.

Miriam searched her mind for an easy way to expose this funny little man's lies. The futility of the entire situation took the form of a cruel presence.

"I still don't understand why you're here. Even if what you're saying is true, why come all this way to speak with a woman you've never met?"

"You're looking for a reason. I understand that, Miriam. A reason for everything. I can assure you; I have my reasons for being here. Your husband told me many things in the time we spent together. Some things he might not have told you. I want to be truthful and direct because you seem like a woman who deserves it. The truth can never be too direct, don't you agree?"

She shook her head and tucked a stray strand of hair behind her ear. The man pressed his lips together in a tight, straight line before offering a cobble-stone smile.

"Soft truth," he continued. "I have no use for soft truth. It's easy to hear. You know the kind, yes? Soft truth is like cheap whisky, Miriam. It makes you sick if you drink too much. Do you see? Direct truth is different. Direct truth might as well be medicine."

It was best not to argue with him. She considered that he might actually be insane. He spoke in circles that dizzied her. When she failed to respond, he seemed satisfied and began fingering the edges of her tablecloth.

"Nice fabric, this cloth. It was expensive, yes?"

Then, his eyes widened.

"Your husband, he knew he would pass. He was not well in the end."

"No, he wasn't."

Miriam thought she saw him relax his shoulders a bit.

"He spoke to me that I should find you after enough time had passed — a few months, maybe. He made me promise to him that I would try. This is why I come here today in this bad weather and in my good shoes."

Miriam pressed her fingertips to her forehead. The rain had slowed again and the drops on her window, tiny beads of nectar, traced shadows on the table.

"What is it that's so important?"

"Would you be so kind as to point me to your restroom? We will discuss about my reasons after. Once we have talked, I'll leave you to go about your day."

She pointed him in the direction of the bathroom, and he tottered clumsily down the narrow passage. Once she knew that he could no longer see her, she slumped forward and pressed her face into her hands. It was true that her husband had been a quiet and reflective man. He rarely spoke about his day, instead favoring to tell Miriam about what he'd read and learned. There was never any small talk. There were no meaningless, mundane questions between the both of them.

For several minutes, the man failed to emerge, but Miriam could hear him puttering somewhere in the apartment. She got up, enraged that this stranger would have the gall to rummage through her belongings. She walked past his stinking, soaked shoes, and found him in the bedroom measuring the bedframe with the roll of measuring tape she kept in her sewing kit.

"I thought it best to go about the business discretely," he said when he noticed her in the doorway.

"My mother, God rest her soul, she told me that most things are best done quietly, you see, so as not to upset people."

He folded up the measuring tape and placed it into his coat pocket.

Then, he stepped back as though to admire the bedroom.

"Yes, this will be fine. It will do just fine. I should say I'll be happy here, Miriam. You wouldn't like my apartment much — an old, drafty place that stinks of cabbage. It's too small for two people and much too small for children. Of course, we will need a larger bed and curtains would do the room nicely. I see now that you have none, and that makes me wonder what kind of a woman undresses at night in a room without curtains."

"Children? Curtains?"

The man looked at her with astonishment.

"I assumed that a bright woman like yourself had figured it out by now, Miriam. Haven't I been obvious? You look to me like an intelligent woman if not a scandalous one who prefers to undress for all to see. Your husband, he makes me promise to come and convince you of marriage. I promised him this when he became ill. You shouldn't be left alone, he told me."

It all happened so quickly, as though she were moving in her sleep. Before she could judge her actions, she realized that she'd knocked the man down to the floor. He sat there in a daze, legs akimbo, with his bloated hand clutching his head. A thin stream of blood flowed from his brow. Miriam's hand burned.

"Leave now," she choked. "You need to leave now and without so much as another word or I'll scream. I swear I will. I'll call the police and tell them I have an intruder."

"This is very unkind of you, Miriam. Very unkind. I wonder now if I should marry a woman with such a temper. But I think of your husband, wise as he was, and I'll extend to you another chance for his sake and for the sake of my mother, who'd always wanted me to marry."

He remained on the floor, a formless mound of clay.

"Leave!"

The exhortation rose from her with such power that it stung her throat. The man, startled, scrambled to his feet, pushed past her, and collected his stinking shoes at the door.

"You've treated me unjustly, Mrs. Smolinsky. You've been very unkind. We can talk of beds and curtains and other such important things another time, but I trust that when I return, you'll be of better humour."

The peculiar man disappeared into the corridor, and the rain returned. Miriam sat down in the doorway, hunched over her knees, and bellowed into the empty quiet of her apartment.

The next day, the rain brought with its departure blue skies, but Miriam's day passed in obscurity. She did not leave the confines of her apartment and instead sat in bed, drinking old tea made from leftover leaves. The odour of the man's shoes lingered in the apartment long after he'd gone. In every room, she felt his presence, his imposing manner, and felt dismayed by the fact that open windows and sunlight couldn't expel his ghost. She woke up at night with a fright, having imagined that he was still sitting at her table, eating her cheese and talking of beds and curtains. But as the days passed, her anger towards him was replaced with comfort in the presence of his imagined ghost. Yes, he'd become familiar to her, as familiar as her own thoughts. She grasped at the memory of his odd voice, listening for the rise and fall as she slept. She worried that he'd never existed.

When she'd run out of food, she collected what little money she had and set out towards the corner store. The sun, a sad disc in the sky, offered no warmth. The city smelled of incoming rain. She had forgotten what it smelled like when the weather turned — crisp, smoky. A couple of children played hopscotch on the pavement, and a woman yelled from an open window for them to get inside before the rain came down.

At the store, Miriam took her time filling her small basket. She pressed the bread the way her mother had taught her, selecting the softest and freshest loaf. Next, she purchased a bag of onions, new potatoes, and a fresh herring with a gaping mouth. She made light and pleasant conversation with the man behind the counter as he calculated her purchases. Outside, grey clouds hung over the city. The rain seemed to start the moment Miriam stepped out the door and it quickly drenched everything in sight. She'd brought neither a coat nor an umbrella. It wasn't long before the rain had saturated her hair and clothes. She walked quickly with her head down and her eyes watching her feet as they splashed against the sidewalk.

"What are you doing out in such rain and without an umbrella? And in your good shoes?"

She looked over at the familiar voice and saw the strange little man with his rounded belly and bulging eye. He sat on a piece of wet cardboard, his back resting against a brick storefront. He still had on his black leather shoes, his woolen coat, and his cobble-stone smile. His beard was a sad, limp fern, and his cheeks seemed hollower than before. Something smelled of rot. She noticed an empty soup tin at his feet with a few coins pasted wetly to the bottom. Rain gathered on her shoulders as they regarded one another. Miriam noticed a large, yellow folder of some sort tucked beneath his coat.

"You've given more thought to my offer," he said. "Nothing but the best for the doctor's widow."

"Scholar," she corrected.

"Ah, yes, Mrs. Smolinsky. Miriam. Fourth-floor apartment, yes? I apologize. My memory, like most things, tires with age."

He muttered something incomprehensible as though recalling a set of instructions.

"I worked with your husband."

"So, you've said."

"Your apartment with three bedrooms will be just fine once I move in."

She shook her head and thought of her small, one-bedroom apartment.

The man sucked on his teeth. Miriam turned to leave but the man, smelling of old socks and death, shot up and grasped her wrist, pulling her back forcefully onto the pavement. She fought against his attempts to restrain her and, in the ensuing struggle, pushed him into the gutter where he landed with a thud, hiding the back of his head against the sidewalk. The tattered yellow folder fell from his coat — strips of newspaper clippings scattered in the wet street and dissolved in the rain. Horrified, Miriam bent over to collect them. She watched as handfuls of obituaries clipped from newspapers lay like limp ribbons in her hands. Among them, a black-and-white photograph of her husband. *Deceased at home. His wife, Mrs. Miriam Smolinsky, without children and thirty-one, has been left a widow.*

Miriam tucked her husband's obituary into her basket beside the wet bread and fish and headed home.

THE SON

Almost one year after they had married, Henry buried his wife. Two days later, he buried his son. Sylvie had gone into labour in the winter. Jobs were scarce, and Henry had been out of work for months. He remembered how she had writhed on their thin mattress, her nightgown pulled up around her waist, while the woman who lived next door rushed around for clean towels and hot water. He couldn't remember the woman's name now; it had already been twenty-two years. He only remembered the gruff way in which she had demanded he stand in the corner so as not to be in the way. Her grasp of English was tenuous at best, and Henry had concentrated on the three, wiry black hairs that sprouted on her pointed chin. She'd smelled of cabbage and was heavy-set. Although he'd hated the way she rushed around and ordered him about, she had been the only option. A winter storm had engulfed the city. It was the worst storm Henry had ever seen; even the streetlights were swallowed up in a blur of wind and snow. He was thankful, at least, that Sylvie had calmed in the woman's presence. He stood in the corner and watched as the heavy Russian patted Sylvie's brow with a cloth, held her hand, and told her to push in broken English.

Night had broken like a fever, and his son was born just as a pale sunlight inched its way across the sky. The Russian gathered the noiseless bundle and placed it into Henry's arms. Then, she had tried to stop Sylvie's bleeding. The newborn choked and sobbed against Henry's chest, Sylvie continued to bleed, and within an hour, she had passed.

Now, Henry could barely recall the colour of his wife's eyes, but he couldn't forget the bluish tint on her skin and the stench of blood coagulating on the bedsheets — the metallic scent of old coins. The smell had remained in their apartment for some time, even after her body had been removed and the bedsheets thrown away.

His son, who he'd refused to name, had been born a withered, frail old man wrapped in a towel. His head, too large for his body, hung on a scrawny neck. He failed to take milk due a split lip cleft upwards toward his nose. He lingered in the hospital for two days and, one morning, the doctor called Henry and announced that his son had passed. It was no great surprise. Henry didn't attend the burial and never spoke of him again.

Now twenty-two years later, Henry felt little when he thought of his son's passing. After all, he hadn't gotten the chance to know him. It was as though the horrid ordeal had happened to someone else — someone who no longer existed. Over the years, he'd refused to marry again and had lived a life of voluntary celibacy. It wasn't that he had passionately loved his wife. He had liked her enough to marry her and, given enough time, they might have settled into some sort of quiet, unassuming love for one another, but he hadn't mourned for long after her passing. His celibacy was merely borne of a distaste for others.

One day, someone pushed a white envelope beneath Henry's door and made a hasty departure. The envelope, blank on the front, stood out like a white stone on his brown doormat. He plucked it from the floor and held it up to the light, examining it as though he might be able to discern its contents without opening it. The letter made him nervous.

He placed it on the kitchen table and boiled water for his tea, occasionally looking at the envelope as though it were a wild animal plotting an escape.

When he'd finished brewing tea, he sat at the table and carefully peeled the top of the envelope. Inside, he found a folded piece of lined paper stained yellow in the upper right-hand corner.

> *I'm not sure whether to begin this letter by addressing you as Henry or Mr. Braum. The first is too informal, I assume. The second feels too formal. I've decided not to address it at all. I'll instead get straight to the point. I would like to meet you as I have something important to discuss. Let's just say that you owe it to me and if you have any remorse for the past, you'll meet me at Cheskie's tomorrow at noon.*
>
> *Best wishes,*
>
> *Alan*

Never in his godforsaken life had he owed anything to anybody, he thought. He crushed the letter in his first and threw it across the room where it landed beneath a coat rack. The word *remorse* bothered him the most. For what could he be remorseful of? What great sin had he committed? He'd always kept to himself.

Although he tried to ignore the wad of paper beneath the coat rack, he couldn't help but think about it. What could this man possibly want? Had the letter been sent to the wrong person? Perhaps there was some other Henry or some other Mr. Braum who had committed some egregious sin, something worthy of repent. He decided then that he would attend the meeting if only to tell the man that he had the wrong Mr. Braum and that he, indeed, owed nobody nothing. He thought about the letter and the meeting for the remainder of the day and, after listening to some old records, took his heavy limbs to bed.

Cheskie's was a small diner a few streets away. He'd only been once or twice. Inside, two young women leaned forward in their chairs, murmuring over steaming cups. He stood at the doorway and watched them for longer than was appropriate before finally locating a two-person table. He could still see the women from where he sat. The more attractive of the two wore her hair up in a high ponytail. She reminded him of his wife, as far as he could remember.

"What can I get for you?"

A waitress with a white apron appeared.

"Coffee," he said, barely looking at her.

"Cream? Sugar?"

"Neither."

The waitress scurried towards the back of the restaurant and disappeared. Henry wondered how he would recognize the author of his letter. Maybe the writer would recognize him? He scanned the room. The women still spoke in hushed tones punctuated occasionally with laughter. An elderly man sat at the front of the diner, straining his eyes at the pages of an open book. Could that be him? No. He decided that the letter had the air of a young man. The waitress reappeared with a cup of coffee.

"Cream? Sugar?" she asked again.

"No."

"What about a pastry? We bake them fresh every morning."

"No."

The coffee tasted alright. He'd had better. When he'd finished half the cup, he looked down at his watch. It was well past noon, and the lunch rush was beginning to thin. Henry sighed upon realizing that his curiosity as to who the letter writer was would likely remain unsatisfied. He'd give it ten more minutes. After that, he'd leave.

Another ten minutes went by, and Henry stood to put on his coat. Just as he stepped away from the table, a tall and lanky man with long arms entered. The man removed his cap and shook snowflakes to the floor. Their eyes met. The man was handsome despite his lanky frame — he had a strong nose, squared shoulders, and a high forehead. He seemed to be somewhere in his twenties and carried with him an air of confidence and responsibility. The man approached and sat opposite Henry. Neither one of them averted their gaze. They merely studied each other, silently. Dishes clanked. A fork scraped against a plate. Henry found himself unarmed; exposed.

"Have you figured out why I'm here?"

His voice wasn't what Henry had imagined. It had a melodious quality to it — sad like a song.

"No. I haven't thought much about it," he lied. "I don't know anybody by your name and now that I see you, I'm even more convinced that you have the wrong Henry; the wrong Mr. Braum."

"I'm certain I have the right person."

"How can you be so sure? If I tell you I've never met you before, then I never have. That's that."

"Look, I've spent a lot of money and a lot of time finding you, your name, and your address. It took me a lot of courage to write you the way I did. The least you could do is accept the fact that you might know me."

Henry felt a curious yet fleeting sense of pity upon hearing that the young man had spent time and money tracking down the wrong person. He shook it off; instead growing angry that the man had pulled him from the warmth of his home on a cold day just to sit and have mediocre coffee.

"I don't know what to tell you."

"You really have no idea who I might be?"

"No."

"I'm your son."

Henry scoffed louder than he'd intended to.

"You don't believe me. I can tell from your face."

"Damned right I don't believe you. Listen, you little shit, I don't have a son, and I sure as hell don't believe you just plopped into existence out of thin air."

"Henry, Mr. Braum…"

"I don't know what kind of scam you're running here, but you ain't running it with me."

Henry slammed his closed fist on the table, pulled his coat back on, and ran from the building — leaving the bill unpaid.

"Let him pay it, the little shit," he muttered to himself as he pulled the collar of his coat against his neck.

He trudged the stainless, powdered streets, his boots sinking a few inches into the accumulated snow as he walked — reminders of desperate steps. When his building finally came into view, he was seized by an overwhelming urge to run back to Cheskie's and listen to what else the young man had to say. But he knew he couldn't turn back. With any luck, he'd never see the man again.

Henry remained agitated for days after the meeting. He now hated his apartment. He hated the way the heater clanked and clacked all night. He hated little things about himself too; things he'd never before noticed — the sounds he made when chewing, the wrinkles that had settled beneath his sagging eyes, the crookedness of his right index finger. Most of all, he hated Alan. He wished he could escape it all and yearned to shake himself free of the heavy Russian, the bedsheets stained with blood, the wailing shriveled infant, the memories that now refused to leave him with even a moment of solace. If only he could free himself of these things, he'd feel a dozen pounds lighter, and he could go on to maybe achieve something with whatever time he had left.

Another week passed during which Henry did little of anything other than shovel driveways and sidewalks for work. One day he+ returned home to find yet another white envelope at his feet. This time, *Henry*, was written on the front of the envelope in neat, cursive penmanship. He tore it open upon entering.

Henry,

I've finally settled on addressing you by your first name. After meeting you, "Mr. Braum" just doesn't feel right. I apologize for upsetting you the way I did, and I'd like a second chance to explain myself if you'd allow it. I confess that I approached the subject rashly and without much consideration for your feelings. I can assure you that this is not a scam. I've sought you out with nothing but the best of intentions. I must close the book on my past, and I can't do this without your help. If you can, please meet me at Cheskie's again tomorrow at noon. I'll be waiting.

Sincerely,

Alan

Henry read the letter twice and decided that there was something sad and pitiful about the man's writing. It must be terrible to leave the past open, to have to live there, but for the life of him he could not figure out why the man would introduce himself as his son. His son had died and anyway, the sickly red infant his wife had given birth to, the one that had lingered for two days in the hospital, could hardly be called his child. Still, Henry decided that the young man desperately needed something. It came to him that the man might be suffering from a delusion or had at the very least been misguided by someone who had taken advantage of his yearning for answers and had produced the name and address of some random person. Either way, Henry felt regret for how he'd reacted during their first meeting. He should have heard him out, at the very least.

As instructed, just before noon the next day, Henry walked to

Cheskie's. It was a pleasant day. The succession of winter storms had ended, and a cold sunlight glistened in the sky. Today was the day he'd find closure and give closure. They'd sit down together, order something to drink, and he'd listen to the man and attempt to give him whatever it is that he needed to move on. Closing the book on one's past is a necessity, he thought.

Cheskie's soon came into view. The large glass window in the front had been cracked. He guessed that it was perhaps the result of the recent winter storms. Perhaps children had launched small pebbles at the glass, an innocent act of vandalism. As he approached, he saw that Alan was sitting at the table just in front of the window. He saw Henry, too, and waved. Sunlight fell upon the long crack that reached diagonally from one corner of the window to the other. A thin shadow rested on Alan's face, giving the impression of a lip cleft up towards a broad nose. Henry turned quickly and in his haste slipped on the ice, slamming the back of his hand on the cold pavement. He woke to the plain waitress kneeling at his side, shaking his shoulder. When he finally stood with the help of the waitress, he looked over at the cracked window and noticed that the table now sat empty. He could only smell the copper-coin stench of old blood.

THE ELEPHANT

Sarah had grown up surrounded by elephants — elephants she'd only seen in the colourful children's' books and illustrated stories that littered the kitchen table and her bedroom floor. A house isn't a home without books, her father had often said. Her first memories were of books. The simplistic stories and carefully etched drawings that made up her childhood only grew more complex with time. Her mother read, too. She kept her books stacked on the coffee table in a neat tower. While her mother preferred self-help books and paperback romance novels, none of which interested Sarah, her father preferred weightier books, old biographies whose pages had yellowed in the sun.

"You think too much," her mother would often tell him. "Life's too short for such thinking. Someday, you'll be on your death bed wishing you hadn't wasted so much time thinking."

Perhaps she was right. But to her father, thinking was a pastime. His mind was a labyrinth of questions that left little room for much else. The largest bookcase in his study — a mahogany case that stretched from floor to ceiling — housed volumes of encyclopedias collecting dust. He'd once set out to read the entire set but had only made it as far as the letter

F before shifting his curiosity to something else. The encyclopedias were quickly abandoned and consigned to the top shelves. His next obsession centered on animals. Books on waterfowl, arctic birds, and entomology whet his appetite for wildlife, but he reserved the top of his desk for his favourite texts. They were small, unremarkable books including *The Asian Elephant: An Action Plan for Its Conservation* and *The Elephant Family*. Sarah remembered these titles more vividly than she remembered most things, often pausing in the doorway to observe them with their well-worn corners.

"Did you know, Sarah, that elephants can live over seventy years."

"Did you know that they sometimes purr to communicate with each other?"

Her mother had little patience for elephants or much else. Thus, Sarah took an interest in them at first to please her father, but later because she'd begun to share his enthusiasm. At her request, her father decorated her bedroom with elephants. It was a small room with a lone window at the far end. He had painted the room a soft shade of pink — her favourite colour — and adorned the walls with framed prints. The first of these prints showcased a watercolour illustration of a smiling elephant spraying a wide stream of water from its trunk down onto the back of her calf. Another was a charcoal sketch of two elephants balancing their massive bodies on circus balls, a faceless audience watching from behind. Her father didn't like this print, as he didn't care much for circuses. Sometimes she'd find him in her bedroom, pondering the sketch with great seriousness.

Her bedroom contrasted greatly with the rest of the house which her mother had decorated in muted light browns and ashy blues. Her mother was a difficult person to know, unlike her father, who spoke to everyone and anyone he encountered, whether it be one of his students or simply a stranger he happened to sit next to on the bus. Sarah, however, knew that her mother's stern, unsmiling face, and quiet nature weren't all there was to her. Her occasional laughter came adorned in sequins and her hugs, though scarce, contained within them a great warmth. She latched onto the religious rituals instilled in her by her own mother, not out of any fervent belief but out of strict adherence to routine. Sarah wasn't certain her mother even believed in God. She recited nightly prayers and blessing from memory with an almost mathematical accuracy. Her lips would carefully sound out the words as though quoting from memory a list of objective, disembodied facts. There was a sadness in her mother that seemed only dissipate during these moments of thoughtless prayer.

On Friday evenings after dinner, Sarah and her father would retire to his study together. Her father would dim the touch-light on his desk, and they'd read together. This was their ritual. Her mother had her prayers, and they had books. When Sarah grew weary of reading, she'd sit at her father's feet, resting her head in his lap, listening as he read from his numerous books. Most often, they ended the evening reading something about elephants. Then, her father would tuck her into her own bed as she gazed at the moon outside her window, hanging like a white oyster shell in the sky.

One Saturday morning, her father woke her before the sun had risen.

"Sarah, guess what?"

"Hmm."

She refused to open her eyes.

"Think good, and it'll be good." I was doing some early-morning reading. Rabbi Menachem Mendel said that. Wake up, your mother is making pancakes."

Think good, and it'll be good. She wasn't sure what that meant, but she somehow felt that it was necessary. Her father had enjoyed an early start to each day. She, however, was a committed sleeper, much like her mother. She went to bed late and would sleep until noon if her father allowed it. He often woke her early, and called sleeping in 'hiding from the day.'

"Life begins in the morning. Even the flowers are unfurling from their sleep as we speak. The earth is opening up, Sarah. Come quickly, or you'll miss it."

That morning, her mother sat three pancakes on her plate and drizzled them with sweet, brown syrup.

"Were you going to tell me something?", Sarah inquired.

She often had to remind him of things he'd meant to say. For as much of a thinker as her father was, conversations darted in and out of his head. He could never grab hold of any of them for too long.

"Ah, elephants," he said, snapping his fingers. "The city zoo is getting one. I read it in the paper this morning. It arrives next week."

"Can we go?"

"Of course. We'll bring your mother."

Her mother scoffed, and her father laughed his characteristic heavy chortle. Whenever her mother pretended to be irritated, she pursed her lips and crinkled her nose.

"This one thinks I have nothing better to do than to stand around and look at stinky animals all day."

"No need to call us names," he chuckled.

Her mother smiled. A genuine smile was rare, but if anything could drag it out of her, it was her husband.

After breakfast, her father marked the elephant's arrival on the calendar pinned by the refrigerator. Seven days. She wondered whether the elephant would be bigger than she imagined it. Would it be as impressive as the elephants in her father's books? She imagined it approaching them from behind the fence. With any luck, it might come close enough for her to reach her hand out and touch its weathered skin.

"Aren't you glad you didn't hide from the day?" her father would ask her.

This time, she would agree.

Every day that week, her father drew a large 'X' on the calendar in red ink. Sarah peppered him with questions, eager to learn everything there was to know about elephants.

"Can elephants swim?"

"Yes, they love to swim."

"Can they feel anything on their thick skin?"

"It's surprisingly sensitive. You wouldn't think it by looking at them, but they can feel even the smallest of insects."

"I can't get away from all this elephant talk," her mother would interject. "I'll never understand this fascination with zoos. Animals don't belong behind fences. What's the point of seeing them in such a place?"

Sarah and her father would nod in agreement if only to avoid further conversation.

On Friday, Sarah headed to school with anticipation for the following day. She stood at the end of her driveway awaiting the school bus, and wondered whether the elephant would be cold in the colourless mists of a cold March morning. Sarah tapped her boot against a small puddle and watched the ripples move across its surface. A chipmunk scurried noisily between bare tree branches, and the sharp, hidden calls of a bird permeated the dense fog. When the bus finally arrived, she settled down into one of the green vinyl seats and rested her cheek against the cold window. Telephone poles, rooftops, and bent trees zipped by, blurring as her breath frosted the glass.

They spoke excitedly over supper that night. Her father gestured as he talked about elephants. Sarah moved and fidgeted in her chair, hardly able to contain herself. After they'd eaten, they washed the dishes and retired to her father's study. Sarah listened as he read from a book of poetry. Sometimes, she understood the poems, but often not. Nevertheless, she closed her eyes and attempted to absorb the way her father carefully pronounced each word of a poem before releasing it into the world. The words, beautiful and free from rigidity, were yet another thing she'd come to depend on — yet another way of hearing God.

They ended their evening earlier than usual. At ten o'clock, her father ushered her to her bedroom, fluffed her pillow, and pulled her bedsheets up over her shoulders.

"Can we play questions?"

"Alright, but just for a few minutes. We have a big day tomorrow."

The question game was something that father had devised one night when she'd been sick and unable to sleep. She would ask him questions, with the aim of finding a question that he couldn't answer. If she succeeded, he'd have no choice but to search for an answer for the next night. The game would end when her father couldn't answer a question or when Sarah fell asleep. It was always the latter.

"What are trees made of?"

"Wood."

"What's wood made of, then?"

"Wood is made of atoms."

"And rocks?"

"They're made of atoms too. Everything is."

"Even elephants?"

"Even us."

She contemplated this and yawned, picturing the tiny atoms abuzz in her body — her fingertips, the ends of her hair, the soles of her feet.

"Time for bed."

He kissed her forehead and turned off the bedside lamp.

"Tomorrow will be a day of good things," he said.

But Sarah didn't dream good dreams. She dreamt of the park down the street from her house, a small park with a rusted swing set and a red plastic slide. In her dream, she sat on the swing, and its chains chirped whenever she swung her legs. Both her father and mother watched as she swung higher and higher. Her mother covered her eyes with her hands and uttered a stiff blessing as her father beamed up at her. The higher she swung, the longer her legs grew. Soon, she found herself up so high that she could no longer see the ground. She could no longer see her parents, the red slide below, or hear her mother's rehearsed blessings. She saw only an expanse of blue sky above and smoky clouds below.

"This isn't the best story to tell, Sarah," her father's voice boomed through the clouds.

And so, she leaped, her elongated legs flailing against the empty space. She jumped, and woke up in her dark, warm bedroom. Outside, she could hear a lone car racing down the wet streets.

"Wake up, Sarah. No sense in hiding from the day."

She hadn't realized she'd fallen back asleep. Her father was leaning against the door frame with a cup of coffee in hand.

"Is Mom up too?"

"Not yet. We should let her sleep."

Once she was dressed and had brushed her teeth, her father brought her a small mug filled half-way with coffee. They stood in the kitchen sipping in silence. Sarah didn't particularly like the taste of coffee, but standing there with her father drinking coffee in the soft morning light made her feel grown up.

They took the bus to the city zoo. Only a few other people got off when the bus stopped. Sarah and her father headed eagerly to the entrance, where a man in a black shirt gave them their tickets.

"What should we see first?" Sarah asked.

"We should build up to the elephant. We won't be impressed with anything else if we see it first. What do you think?"

She nodded, and they went in the direction of the petting zoo. Sarah spent a while feeding a white goat from the palm of her hand while her father scattered seeds for the ducks that congregated at his feet. Then they moved on to the parrots with their kaleidoscope plumage, followed by the lion exhibit. Unfortunately, most of the lions were napping, and apart from the occasional sharp-toothed yawn, they remained unaware of their spectators. Sarah's thoughts were consumed by the elephant as they passed a jungle-gym of monkeys, two female zebras in a gated area, and a couple of foxes pacing their enclosure.

"What do you say we go see the elephant now?"

Sarah nervously agreed; days' worth of anticipation had led to this. On their way to the elephant enclosure, they paused to look at the gorillas. A large male picked at a pile of fruit, while two smaller females groomed each other nearby, paying little attention to Sarah and her father. They paid little attention to Sarah and her father. The elephant would be different, she told herself.

The elephant was hidden behind a tall, wooden fence. Sarah's father hoisted her up onto his shoulders. She barely noticed the elephant at first; it hardly moved. A large, rusty chain was wrapped snugly around its rear leg, granting just enough length for the elephant to reach a mound of hay in the center of the small enclosure. Apathetic, the elephant did not look at her audience. Multiple piles of wet droppings dotted the thin grass and brown mud where she stood. The backs of her sunbaked legs were caked in a thick layer of feces, which occasionally dribbled down and dried to her skin. Her trunk grabbed listlessly at the individual clumps of hay. Sarah could see the angular presence of her hip bones.

"I wish she'd look at us," remarked a young boy standing next to Sarah and her father.

Someone in the crowd whistled, but the elephant didn't turn her head. Sarah thought of the tall, majestic animals she'd see in her father's books. She thought of their bright and curious eyes, their bodies robust, and their legs free to roam. This elephant bore no resemblance to the ones she'd seen in those books. Long, leathery scars snaked like rivers across her back. One of the wounds, oozing fluid and buzzing with flies, seemed fresh. The elephant simply occupied space — a sad, gaunt animal in a muddy enclosure. When someone hurled a pebble into the enclosure, the elephant strained against her chain, attempting to move forward in vain.

Sarah shut her eyes as her father helped her down off his shoulders.

"Can we go home?"

"I think that might be best."

On their way out, Sarah looked around at all the exhibits and the animals trapped within them. The gorilla still picked unenthusiastically at the pile of rotting fruit; his eyes downcast as he peeled an orange. The lions, who at first glance had seemed comfortable and content slumbering atop the large stones in their enclosure now seemed to her sad, stretched atop wet, uneven boulders. They shifted their bony frames closer to each other for warmth. She couldn't help but see the missing patches of feathers on the parrots who had plucked themselves out of boredom.

"Come again soon," said the ticket man in the black shirt.

They listened to the country songs that played on the bus, kept their eyes fixed to the floor, and wished time away.

Sarah barely noticed her mother's presence as she burst through the front door and ran to her bedroom, where she ripped the framed elephant prints from her wall and hid them in her closet behind a pile of dirty laundry.

"What happened?"

Her mother opened the door and came in, much to Sarah's disappointment. She wished it had been her father.

"Sarah?"

Her mother's voice seemed subdued.

"Did you take your pictures down?"

"Yes."

"It wasn't what you expected it would be, was it?"

Sarah felt her mother's small but firm hand on her back.

"Nobody has all the answers, Sarah."

It was her only attempt at comfort, and she soon left. Sarah slept.

"I wanted to say goodnight."

Her father woke her just as the sky had dimmed with the solemnity of dusk. His tone was sedate, his voice low. He sat on the edge of her bed and kissed her hair.

"I don't know, Sarah. I just don't know."

That was all she needed.

HOUSE OF MIRRORS

The carnival came to town the year that Albert turned sixteen. It had been a year marked by growing restlessness; the things that had once mattered to him no longer did. Most of that summer, he whiled away the hours drinking stolen beers by the river. It was better than staying home and watching his father drink himself to sleep and his mother slowly unraveling. Would this be it? A life spent watching waves of expanding heat rise in the distance. As far as he was concerned, 1941 had been a shit year. Germany had attacked the Balkans, and there was a surprise attack on a U.S. fleet at Pearl Harbor. He wasn't sure whether he should care about any of it.

The carnival, at least, was something to do. On the night before it packed up to move on to some other distant town, Albert counted a fistful of change he'd taken from the till in his father's convenience store. His father had owned the store for a decade, and Albert had spent every summer helping him out. He hated that store. He hated the aisles lined with unsold canned goods that nobody ever bought, the clanging sound the register made whenever he opened its drawer, the tedium of checking inventory, stacking cartons of eggs, packages of toilet paper, and restocking the seemingly sole item that people ever bought — beer.

Thinking about his future, which at that moment felt like no real future at all, he pocketed the change and headed for the door. In the dimly lit dining room, his mother was hunched over a pile of papers, and his father lay sprawled on the living room sofa, his mouth hanging open. As Albert rode his bike down the street, he wondered what he might do once he'd graduated. He figured that college wasn't an option, nor was it really something he wanted to do. In all likelihood, he'd probably end up working for his father and eventually take over the convenience store himself. He doubted he could resurrect the old building, build it back up to what it had once been. He wondered whether he, too, would end up as a bloated old man, half-asleep on the living room sofa, clutching a bottle of lukewarm beer.

When the Ferris Wheel came into sight, he hesitated. There it stood — a colossal, spinning wheel — a monster, its lights casting ghosts in the night, its ugly music an ominous warning. He stood there and watched the wheel's rotations — spinning, spinning, spinning — with tiny blue and red gondolas hanging like ornaments. A slow, tepid wind blew, and for a fleeting moment, Albert contemplated returning home to his sleeping father and disintegrating mother. A group of children darted past him. Realizing he had nothing to lose, he handed a quarter to the woman at the ticket booth and proceeded through the entry gate.

Inside dusty, worn faces loudly proclaimed chances to win brightly coloured stuffed animals. People weaved past him, their sticky hands clutching wads of cotton candy. Near one of the hotdog stands, a pitiful stray with a limp leg licked at a puddle of what looked to be melted ice cream. Nobody paid the dog any attention. A truck backfired, and the dog ran off. All the while, the Ferris Wheel loomed over him, casting its long shadows across the carnival lot. It watched him. Admonished him. He tilted his head upward and gazed at the towering, metal behemoth. Albert joined the queue along with others waiting their turn. The ride came to a halt, and people slowly exited. When the operator opened the gates, Albert took the first gondola he saw, a red one that swayed as he settled in.

As more people filled the gondolas, Albert felt his stomach lurch. The gondola just ahead of him creaked, and he was seized by a sudden fear that the world would fall out from under him once he reached the top. He attempted to steady his breath, shut his eyes tightly, and gripped the sides of the gondola. His fingers ached miserably, and he counted five complete rotations before the ride stopped, and he was back on solid ground.

He felt it had been a half-hearted attempt, one among many. The Ferris Wheel had felt so necessary to him when he first arrived, but he hadn't seen anything, hadn't felt anything other than a virulent desire to get it over with, his feet aching for solid ground. Convinced he would be unable to salvage the night, he bought himself a bag of popcorn and made his way to the exit gate.

"Come one, come all," a woman's voice called from a darkened booth near the exit. "Discover what your future holds."

Albert wasn't entirely certain whether he'd imagined her voice. The booth seemed abandoned, set so far away from the others, without lights or decorations giving any sign of life. As he neared the booth, he smelled stale cigarettes, the kind of smell that clings to clothes and turns sour with time. His eyes quickly adjusted to the darkness, revealing an older woman seated in the booth — fifty years old, at least. She wore a deep purple dress decorated with silver-embroidered flowers around the neckline. The dress was low-cut. On her arms, bangles — silver with little bells — beckoned to him with their simple, jangling music.

"What does your future hold for you, young man?"

She smiled a smile of yellowed teeth and red lipstick.

"What's your name? I can read your palm if you'd like."

"I don't have any money left," Albert lied.

She motioned for him to approach.

"What's your name?"

"Albert."

"Albert," she repeated.

He studied the lines on her face. She wore her years in the corners of her eyes.

Before he could react, she grasped his wrist and drew his hand forward. With a thin index finger, she carefully traced the length of his palm.

"You're destined for great things."

"Like?"

"You'll see. But you'll be happy. You're in love, yes?"

"In love?"

He turned the question in his mind. Love was something he didn't know much about.

"Too much innocence isn't good either," she whispered, leaning over the front of the booth.

Something shameful stirred within him as he looked down at the tiny, embroidered flowers along her neckline.

"I can tell you all about innocence. If it's important to you, I'll be in the house of mirrors before closing."

Albert nodded. She released his hand. As he walked away from her booth, he had the impression that he'd both escaped something yet had drawn nearer to it at the same time. He purchased a soda and sat on the bench opposite the house of mirrors, seriously considering leaving for he had no idea what he expected. He studied the mural painted across the front of the house of mirrors, covered in faded clown faces.

In less than an hour, he caught sight of her long purple dress and dangling bracelets. She didn't acknowledge him, only entered the house of mirrors and disappeared into the dark. Albert followed. The interior was a ridiculous attraction filled with rippling, lopsided mirrors that stretched and twisted his reflection in different ways.

Before his eyes had the chance to adjust to the growing darkness, he felt her reach for his hand and, without hesitation, he interlaced his fingers with hers. It had been natural, effortless. She pulled him to a spot where only thin rivulets of light filtered in through the cracks in the walls. Mirrors jutted out and receded, curved, twisted, and turned. Neither of them spoke. Albert heard the jingling of her small, silver bells as she pressed her body to his, his back to one of the mirrors, her steady hands undoing his belt.

Their partially clothed bodies bulged and swelled vulgarly in the tilted mirrors as she took him in her hand and guided him into her. When it was over, she pulled her body from his, adjusted her skirt, and left. In that solitary moment, alone with his own reflection, he felt changed, as though something essential had been taken from him. What exactly she had stolen, he couldn't say, but he felt himself lighter from the loss.

People had already started to leave the carnival by the time Albert exited the house of mirrors. He again approached the Ferris Wheel.

"Last ride," the operator announced.

Only a handful of others lined up for the ride. The operator opened the gate, and Albert again sat down in the first gondola he saw. He inhaled the cool summer night air and held it in his lungs for as long as he could. Then, he exhaled, closed his eyes, and felt himself ascend. When the ride paused, he opened his eyes and saw himself perched high above the carnival. Below, people resembling miniscule insects scuttled about, and lights from faraway houses, like forgotten stars, blinked lifetimes away.

One by one, the carnival lights flickered out, and Albert descended to earth.

CORMANY STREET

John had always loved the little white house. His wife had loved it, too. She'd been the first to notice it. Despite its need for renovation, its sun-faded blue shutters and cracked cobblestone pathway held a rustic charm, exactly what they had been hoping for in the early years of their marriage. Only a week into their marriage, she had noticed it during her drive home. She told him that night that she knew it was 'the one', and though he initially thought it cliché, he couldn't deny it when he saw it. It was perfect, but there was no way they could afford it.

Phyllis worked part-time in a perfume factory while taking night courses to obtain her high school diploma. John worked full-time at a local plastics factory, overseeing the production line. Together, their earnings covered the rent for a small one-bedroom apartment in the town's south side. They occasionally discussed children but always decided against it. It was a conversation not worth having then, but the house was something they could both envision. They made it a goal to save as much as possible so that they could someday move into the white house on Cormany Street.

As time passed, however, John grew increasingly restless and frustrated with Phyllis. He felt suffocated, and by the time she'd obtained her diploma, he had already made up his mind to leave her. So many things tore at him — her encroaching presence, her unyielding affection for him, her chirpy singsong voice, and her habit of carelessly leaving the lights on made his ears hot. They shared that cramped apartment, where the pipes froze in the winter, for five years. For five years, John chewed his inner cheek. Then, the day following their wedding anniversary, John packed his boxes and filed for divorce. Any guilt he felt at leaving her was fleeting and quickly replaced with indifference. He thought himself free of her. The small white sores he'd chewed into his own cheek quickly healed. He could think of no better way to punish her unintentional failings than to buy the house on Cormany himself.

Phyllis remained in town, living in their former apartment on a secretary's salary. John felt a perverse satisfaction in calling her when he finally closed on the house. He listened to her voice drop — a sickeningly sweet achievement — and counted it as retribution for the years he'd put up with her. He was lucky that the house had remained on the market — kismet, he thought.

On moving day, he admired the beauty of the bent old maple tree that extended over the front yard. Its autumn leaves had already changed from green to scarlet; its leaves were strewn across the lawn and sidewalk like scattered amber stones. The real-estate agent handed him the keys, and he knew that he'd be happy there. His separation from Phyllis and the purchase of the house marked a significant shift — it signified the shedding of a skin that had for so long constricted him. As soon as his new furniture had been set just the way he liked it, and most of the boxes were unpacked, he settled onto the comfortable living room couch and admired the bare walls. He thought for a while about how he'd like to decorate it, knowing that the decision belonged solely to him. He pictured paintings of sailboats being tossed about by turbulent waves. He'd always loved the sea, something Phyllis had never cared for. To spite her, he decided to paint the living room taupe and the dining room beige. Feeling justified in his anger, he finally went to bed in his new home and slept soundly for the first time in six years.

His first morning was golden, with light filtering between what was left of the precariously hanging maple leaves outside his bedroom window. After stretching, he looked down from his second-floor window and saw a man sitting on the low brick wall surrounding the front yard. The man's back was hunched, and a plastic bag filled with bottles sat beside him. His head was a crown of thick, silver hair. John watched for a while, attempting to ignore his rising bad temper. But the longer he observed the old man, the more upset he became, and by the end, his good mood had vanished.

The man, unmoving and unaware of John's displeasure, stared at the patch of trees across the street. Occasionally, he would reach over to reposition his bag of bottles and rub his arms to warm them against the autumn wind. His green windbreaker was worn, frayed, and unraveling at the seams. The old man's posture conveyed his advanced age. John wondered where the man had come from and what he could possibly want.

After he'd taken the time to dig the coffee maker out of one of the remaining unpacked boxes and had finished drinking his first cup, he again looked out the window. The man was still there. It had been at least half an hour. John considered approaching him but decided against it. No use filling a new morning in a new home with such tension.

The day passed uneventfully, and John kept himself busy unpacking the remaining boxes. He placed knickknacks on shelves, organized his record collection, and found and tossed away a package of photographs from his wedding day. He avoided the window until he couldn't any longer. The man was gone. John exhaled noisily and hoped he wouldn't return. For the next three days, the short brick wall stood unoccupied, collecting fallen leaves.

On the fourth day of his new life, John woke to thoughts of his ex-wife. He lay in bed and tried to remember the reasons he'd fallen in love with her, or whether he had ever loved her at all. He knew that at one point, he had cared enough of her to marry her. It didn't take him too long to realize that he had indeed loved her, once, for the same reason he hated her now — because she loved him. He thought of his past, his marriage, discarded like a pile of broken, forgotten bottles. It had no bearing on who he was now.

When John finally stood up, he felt the skin on his shoulders prickle. He looked out from the window and saw the old man again perched on the wall. There he was with his stooped shoulders, a plastic bag full of bottles, and a frayed windbreaker. Yet what had once enraged John now frightened him. What could this man want? He sensed that perhaps the man wanted something, needed something. Whatever it was, John knew that he could not and would not provide it. John descended the stairs, his footsteps heavy with indignation, and opened the front door to the earthy scent of mid-autumn.

"Hey," he called out.

The old man paid him no attention.

"Hey, old man," John raised his voice.

Startled, the man jumped and turned to look at John.

"Time to move on. Get off my property. This is the second time I've seen you here, and I think you should know that I bought the house. I don't want you here on my property."

The old man had a gaunt face — dark, sunken eyes and a thin nose. His ashy skin was even more wrinkled than John had imagined it. Sickened at the sight of him, John slammed the door shut and tried to suppress any growing feeling of sympathy. He watched from the window as the old man collected his bag of bottles and walked away. Feeling a misbegotten sense of accomplishment, John went about his day content.

September and October passed in relative peace. Sometimes, John thought of the old man and wondered whether he'd overreacted. He also wondered how Phyllis was getting along in the old apartment they'd shared for six years. The past was the past.

In late November, the first snow fell and covered his windows in wintry lace. Moonlight sparkled on the thin sheet of snow covering the browned maple leaves. The air carried with it the subtle scent of an oncoming storm, but the storm never arrived, just feathery flakes that glittered in the night. Around midnight, John saw a darkened figure perched on the brick wall. This time, he stepped out into the snow. The street was quiet, all sounds muted by winter's arrival.

"If you don't go away, I'll call the police," he said gruffly.

The man remained silent. After a few moments, he collected his bag of bottles, and his footprints were quickly erased by the falling snow.

Worried that the man might continue visiting his property, John decided to phone his real-estate agent. He hoped she knew something, anything, about the man.

"You've reached Superior Realty; this is Jean. How can I help you?"

"Jean, it's John."

"John?"

"I purchased the house on Cormany this past autumn," he explained.

"Yes, John! Are you settling in nicely? Quite a bit of snow we've gotten already."

"I'm settling in just fine. Thank you. I have an odd question."

"Go ahead. I'm here to help."

John hesitated.

"There's a man that comes by here occasionally. He's older and sits on the wall bordering my property. I'm not sure what he wants, and I was wondering whether you knew anything about him."

"I see," she said.

"I figured maybe he'd come around before I moved in. Did the previous owners say anything?"

"Well," she finally replied. "I noticed him once when I stopped to check the property. It was only once. At least, I think it was him. He wasn't doing much other than sitting there, and I didn't have the heart to tell him to leave. He looked harmless enough. Has he been bothering you?"

"Yes."

"How so?"

"He's been threatening me. I think he's up to no good," John lied.

"Has he done anything?"

"No, not really. He sits there in the snow like an idiot. But I tell you, he's been threatening me."

"If he's threatening you, I suggest you call the police. On my end, the previous owners never mentioned him, and I only saw him that one time. There's not much more I can do. I'd leave him alone or else call the police. Is there anything else I can help you with today?"

"No. Thank you."

John hung up the phone. A desperate emptiness settled in him. His once comfortable home now felt cavernous — the yawning maw of some sharp-toothed beast. Memories of Phyllis and thoughts of the old man refused to leave him. He tried to cast them both into the past but failed. He wanted to hate them. Hate was comfortable and justified. Hate was palpable. But now, he couldn't grasp it, and that was the most frightening thing of all. If in his present state, he could no longer maintain his detest of Phyllis's neediness or the old man's persistence, he could no longer confine them to the past. They'd become his present, and that he couldn't stand for.

The storm he had sensed for days finally arrived in a blustering sweep. A hostile wind moaned and by early afternoon, six inches of snow had fallen. John went outside to shovel the walkway and sunk into snow that reached halfway to his knees. For thirty minutes, he squinted against a storm that alternated between stinging gusts of snow and pellets of ice.

The snowfall finally slowed after he'd finished shoveling the walkway. Thick flakes still swirled about but did not blow with the same ferocity. In the diminishing storm, John could see the familiar silhouette of a bent old man sitting in the snow.

Exhausted from shovelling and struggling to find any motivation to argue, John conceded defeat and approached the shadowed figure. He sat down beside the bag of bottles and stared ahead at the trees, the very same trees that the old man apparently found so fascinating. But all John saw were old, gnarled trees, their tendril-like branches standing tall against a moonless sky.

"What do you need? Why do you keep coming back here when I've told you not to?"

The old man did not respond.

"What is it that you need?" John repeated, his patience rubbing thin.

Silence.

"Are you mute? Deaf? Dumb? Answer me!"

The old man turned to face John, revealing deep blue eyes. The man looked even more gaunt and worn since John had last seen him. Tears collected in corners of the man's eyes.

"Ever feel like there's something you need to return to? You keep coming back, and it's never what you expect?"

John wasn't sure what the old man meant. He shook his head.

"I like to collect bottles there," the old man said, pointing up the street.

John waited for him to continue.

"At first, I only stopped here to sit and rest. Then, I felt I had to. There's something, something I keep waiting for and returning to."

"Well, what on earth is it?" John pressed.

The man shrugged his bent shoulders.

"I don't want to be a bother. I'm restless, is all. Nothing but a restless old man. I have regrets, and they keep me up at night. I can't leave things in the past, I guess."

John studied the man's grief-stricken eyes and winter-reddened nose. An excruciating realization seized him, a harrowing and cruel epiphany. As though looking into a mirror, he saw his own bent shoulders, his own face lined with regret, his own eyes reddened with rage and anguish. The realization mangled him.

"I don't want to be no bother," the old man added. "I'll try not to come back here."

With that, the wintry spectre collected his bag, brushed the snow from his shoulders, and slowly limped away into the storm. John followed him from a distance, until they were both consumed by the snowstorm on Cormany Street.

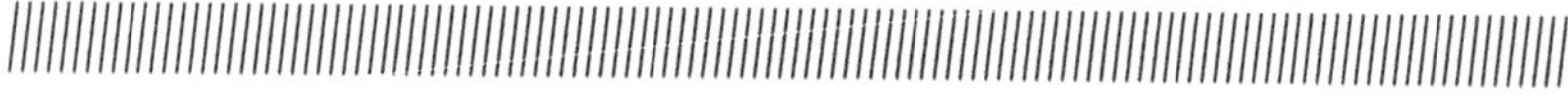

BOXES

Years ago, in a college class that she now barely remembered, Rosalie had read a poem. She didn't remember the author, the professor, or the point of the class. What she did remember was the title, along with the first stanza.

> *She wanted a little room for thinking;*
> *but she saw diapers steaming on the line,*
> *a doll slumped behind the door.*

She could still recite it from memory, and she remembered how small it had made her feel even then, even before she'd considered marriage, even before she'd exchanged blackboards and textbooks for piles of laundry on the basement floor. Now she hated thinking of it. She tried to avoid remembering the poem as she lay awake beside William. She'd never had children and had been apathetic about them as far back as she could remember. But William had wanted them. He'd told her so on their second date. Charmed by his sweet nature and at least moderate attractiveness, she convinced herself that with time, she'd develop the same desire for children. But three years had passed since their wedding night, and her feelings remained unchanged despite William's insistence that they start trying for a family. They spent months trying, and every negative pregnancy test seemed to steal a part of her, leaving her thirsting for air. Whenever she thought she might be pregnant, the poem came to mind — a little room for thinking, a doll slumped behind the door. As each month brought another negative pregnancy test, she considered the idea that she might be infertile. She feigned disappointment, and William treated her as if she might break. Once, she'd confessed feeling broken, and he took this to mean what he wanted, although she meant something she kept to herself.

The truth, the truth that kept her up at night, was that she barely knew William. Despite being married for three years and together for four, she still felt him to be a stranger. She knew the basics: he was a carpenter, he loved her roasted chicken, he liked making love face-to-face, he preferred her with her hair loosely curled and worn down. Beyond that, her knowledge of him dwindled. She might as well be sharing her life with a cardboard cut-out from the grocery store.

Despite there being no doll slumped behind the door and no diapers steaming on the laundry line, she still craved a little room for thinking. She often felt sluggish, tired of doing nothing, her limbs tingling as though slowly dissolving like sand sifting to the bottom of an hourglass. Her youthful dreams of teaching prose and poetry, which had once held so much promise, now felt naïve.

On mornings when William worked, she'd wake an hour before him and prepare his breakfast — toast and eggs sunny-side up. Lifeless. Limp. With her threads pulled and her button eye missing, she'd place the plate on the table beside his morning paper. Then, she'd pass the day mindlessly rearranging pictures on shelves, wiping surfaces with Lysol, and watering the wilted houseplants she couldn't bring herself to throw away. When William stayed home, she nonetheless felt alone. She'd sleep past dawn and take her time with his breakfast, which he unfailingly appreciated. Nothing ever changed. That is until she woke one morning to find that something was missing.

It was a physical sensation, a palpable absence. A crisp autumn light glowed on the cherry-wood bedroom floor, and she smiled at the colour of it despite the dull ache she felt in her right inner thigh. Thinking she must have slept in an odd position; she massaged her inner thigh and hoped the discomfort would pass.

For breakfast, she cracked the last two eggs into an oiled pan and watched as the edges browned to a crisp.

That's when she first felt it — a heavy, intense nausea. The pain in her thigh returned, tearing at her tender skin. When she saw one of yolks break, spilling forth its viscous fluid, she ran to the sink, vomiting bile. Then, she collected herself and forked the eggs with their congealed, spilled yolks onto a plate. She rarely became ill and couldn't remember the last time she'd thrown up. Her mouth filled with thick saliva, and she bent over the sink again, sour bile burning her throat.

William rushed down the stairs upon hearing her retching. He rubbed her back as she continued to gag, her efforts only producing air. When her nausea had lessened, he wrapped her in a blanket and sat her down on the sofa.

"I can call out from work. Do you need anything? Water?"

She shook her head and closed her eyes.

"Go to work. I'll be fine. I think it's just a twenty-four-hour bug. You really shouldn't worry about it."

William fetched her a glass of ice water before he left and placed it on the living room table. He then fluffed her pillow and pressed the back of his hand against her forehead to check for fever, finding none.

Rather than get up and complete her usual chores, she pulled the blanket up to her chin and tried to rest. She tried to remember that she existed, that she was more than furniture, more than a doll with pulled threads. She swallowed her spit and tried not to get sick again. The blanket wrapped tightly around her was warm, and she imagined herself within the confines of a rigid cocoon, her body slowly melting into a pulpy mess only to someday emerge something different. Something beautiful. She concentrated on this feeling, attempting to distract herself from the churning in her stomach. She focused on the blanket's heaviness and the way it felt on her body. She concentrated on her chest, her small breasts, envisioning that once she cast the blanket from her body, she'd be someone new. She'd surface with brighter eyes and supple skin to replace the tired look she carried around. As she felt her cheeks with her fingertips, she found that her skin remained unchanged. Disappointed, she tried her best to sleep.

In the evening, William returned with a bouquet of daffodils and a thermometer he had purchased at the drug store.

"Dinner?" he asked. "I could fix some soup."

"No, thank you, dear. I still don't have much of an appetite."

"You poor thing. Drink your water and get some rest. If you're hungry later, I'll fix you something to eat."

He kissed her parched lips.

"You feel a little warm. Should I take your temperature?"

She declined and said she'd take a cool shower just in case. He helped her up the stairs to the bathroom, where she once again heaved painfully into the toilet.

"Drink," he said as he pressed a cool glass of water to her lips.

She sipped it, and after a few moments, William left.

She knew that she was fortunate to have a husband who cared for her when she was ill. Yet, she couldn't help but feel annoyed at his almost maternal concern for her, as though he didn't trust her to care for herself. She resented being coddled, followed, and fussed over. If only she could find a little room for thinking.

For the remainder of the night, William sat up with her. He brought her cold washcloths until her fever broke, offered her plain saltines to settle her stomach, and gave her Tylenol for the pains that wracked her bones. She dreamed terrible, erratic visions — dreams of boxes lining bright and endless white corridors. Boxes stacked against walls, reaching up towards the high ceilings. Boxes, hanging and swaying overhead on thin thread. Sometimes, she'd reach up, pluck one down like ripe fruit, and open it only to find it empty.

She woke just before dawn to find that she had sweated through the linen sheets. A slice of persistent moonlight still lingered effortlessly, pasted against the dim sky. She rubbed the sleep from her eyes. The nausea was still there, though less severe. She took her temperature and was relieved to find that she was no longer feverish. She longed to fall back asleep and return to her dream, to the empty cardboard boxes. Carefully, she concentrated on the feeling of the warm, cocoon-like blanket and tried to distract herself from the ache in her stomach. William kissed her on the mouth and ran his hand over her hair.

"I'm glad to see that you look a little better. Do you feel better?

"A little," she said.

"Would you like me to stay home today?"

"No, I'll be ok."

"Are you sure?"

"Yes."

When he left for work, she watched his car drive away — an unfamiliar man in a familiar red car.

Upstairs in the bathroom, she shed her clothes to the floor and turned on the hot water. The bathroom was soon shrouded in a white, hot mist. She wiped the fog from the full-length mirror to reveal her naked body. Something was missing. She'd been unable to figure it out the day before in her feverish state. But now, she looked at herself and carefully moved her hand over the hair between her legs, the soft swell of her hips, the dip in her waist. She paused to cup her breasts in her palms. Then, frowning, she allowed the steam to obscure her naked body.

It was only when she'd finished her bath and had begun towelling herself dry that she finally realized exactly what had gone missing. She had undergone an almost microscopic change that would without a doubt have been overlooked by anyone other than herself. A simple birthmark the size of a pencil eraser had vanished. It had been a solitary brown freckle on her right inner thigh. The idea that some part of her, no matter how small, could be pulled away by the moon only to be eaten up by the first light of morning concerned her greatly. She felt a certain sadness, and an inevitable grief for it. She had hated the freckle, and she remembered how she had cringed the first time William kissed it, the first time his lips had moved from the freckle to between her legs. She'd felt nothing. She still felt nothing. That night, still wracked with nausea and worry, she wore pyjama pants rather than a nightdress and hoped that William would never notice — that he'd somehow forget the small chocolate smudge on her inner thigh.

Days later, she had settled into her sickness. Her stomach still churned, but she did her best to eat and keep the food down. She feigned wellness whenever William smiled at her. She tried to move her ragdoll arms and legs and bring life to her button eyes. Thinking she had recovered, William left her with a small grocery list before heading to work. She stared at the list and crumpled it into her pocket.

The day felt heavy. She put on her thickest clothing and opened her umbrella against the rain. In the driveway, she coughed into her fist until a wad of phlegm dislodged itself from her throat. She spit the small ball of blood-tinged mucus on the ground between her feet.

"Rosalie!"

Her neighbour, Eleanor, was waving from her porch.

"How have you been?" Rosalie asked.

"Oh, just fine. I haven't seen you in a while. I was beginning to think that something was wrong."

Eleanor wore a knee-length brown coat and short, close-toed kitten heels. Her red hair frizzed in the autumn rain.

"I've just been a bit busy with the house. You know how it is. William works a lot."

"Oh, trust me, I know how it is. It's enough to drive you crazy. Other than that, you've been alright?"

She shrugged.

"I was sick for a while. It was the flu, I think. I'm beginning to feel better."

"Well, feel free to stop by any time," Eleanor said with a small laugh.

Rosalie rushed inside and took off her coat and boots before she remembered the balled-up grocery list in her pocket. She wanted desperately to stay home. William would surely understand. He always did. She'd simply tell him that she'd fallen sick again. They could make it another day without milk, bread, and eggs. That was it, then. The groceries could wait, and she needed a shower.

She again stripped her clothes and commenced a close examination of her body. Something else had changed — something more noticeable than a mole missing from her inner thigh. She'd lost weight. How had she lost such weight in such a short amount of time? The illness must have been more severe than she'd imagined. Her hips, which once curved softly against her hands, were now sharp — the bones protruding at crude angles. If she turned at a certain angle, she could clearly see the outline of her ribs poking out from beneath anemic skin. She sank to the floor, felt the urge to cry, but found that she had no tears. She choked dryly into her open hands.

William arrived that evening to a cold oven, an empty table, and an unfulfilled grocery list. Rosalie approached him as soon as he walked through the door. With frantic energy, she wrapped her arms around his neck and shook.

"William, something is horribly wrong."

He held her and kissed the top of her head.

"We can call a doctor tomorrow," he offered.

"I don't feel terribly ill anymore. But, William, something is wrong. Don't you see it? Don't you notice something different?

He held her at arm's length and quickly looked her over.

"You're as beautiful as always," he said. "If that's what all this is about, then nothing has changed. You're beautiful, and I've always thought so."

"It isn't about that. It isn't about that at all. You don't see it, do you?"

"Sweetheart, if it really worries you. Let's make an appointment with the doctor tomorrow. It'll put your mind at ease, but I'm sure it's just the flu. You just need more rest, is all. Things will be back to normal soon, you'll see. You'll go back to cooking and reading and doing all the things you like."

Defeated, Rosalie agreed. Perhaps he was right. That night, William once again called her beautiful before he climbed between her legs. She wasn't at all surprised when, after he entered her, she didn't feel anything. Rosalie accepted that this was just another part of her in a series of pieces that had and would eventually disappear. Yes, she would become accustomed to it, accustomed to losing parts of herself, accustomed to watching helplessly as they inched away — parts of her afloat somewhere just out of reach.

"You see," William whispered when he'd finished. "Everything is the same. Nothing has changed."

But it wasn't the same. She now knew that he would never be capable of realizing it. He'd never notice her drifting away, dismantled piece by piece, straying further from herself. She would simply carry on as she was until that inevitable moment when she would vanish completely without notice — the last of her carried away by moonlight.

That night, she dreamed again. The boxes were bigger this time. In that white corridor, she was but a presence perpetually wandering and opening boxes, hoping desperately to find something within them.

THE WALLET

It was a brown stain in the white snow. It caught Normand's attention out of the corner of his eye as he walked along Fraser Street one blustery afternoon. He'd been on his way to pay a visit to a long-time friend of his when, upon seeing it, he came to a complete stop. Overnight, the city had been dusted in white. A strong wind blew the snow about in dizzying whirls, often making it difficult to see anything but shadows of cars and buildings standing guard on street sides. All that stood out to him was that brown wallet half-sunken into a mound of snow just outside Boudreau's hair salon. Only its upper corner peaked out, and he eyed it as though it were discarded treasure. Such an impression it made on him that he took the time to dig it out of the snow, holding it like a small animal between his chilled fingers. It was made of leather, and he could tell based on its faded sides and the tear down the middle that it wasn't new. It was worn and held a history all its own. After turning it over in his hand, he decided that it must belong to someone, for he could not conceive of the idea that someone had knowingly discarded it. Even if it was old, it was still useable. He thought first of the hair salon. It made the most sense that the wallet, lodged in the snow just outside the front door, would belong to someone inside.

He struggled to pull the door open. Three inches of snow had blown against the doorway, and nobody had bothered to shovel it before opening shop. Inside were two women who Normand assumed to be in their mid-twenties. The stylist, a middle-aged woman with greying hair, wore a thick woollen dress with a black apron tied tightly around her waist. Her hair had been dyed brown, but a length of gray roots had grown out, declaring her age. The stylist hadn't acknowledged his arrival as she was concentrating, in a trance-like state, on the young woman who sat in her chair. She carefully ran a wide-toothed comb through strands of thick hair before wrapping them around hot rollers. Normand cleared his throat. The other woman, who sat with a wet head beneath one of the dryers, looked his way.

"Rose, someone's here," she said.

The stylist came out of her trance, looked over to Normand, and frowned. Her fingers continued piecing through the woman's hair as though the motions, over time, had become automatic.

"Can I help you?"

Normand felt he'd stumbled upon a scene he shouldn't have — something private and guarded. He again cleared his throat, forgetting the reason for his presence. Then, remembering why he'd come, he held the wallet up as though offering a gift.

"I found this out in the snow. I thought it might belong to somebody in here since it was right outside."

The young woman beneath the hairdryer shook her head, as did the one with a head half full of hot rollers. Rose furrowed her brows and continued frowning. Normand took her scowl to mean that the wallet did not belong to her or anyone else who happened to be there. Embarrassed, he excused himself and stepped back out into the frosted city.

While he walked, the wallet weighed in his pocket like a handful of stones. He couldn't figure out why it bothered him. Before he had retrieved it, it had just been a menacing stain in the white snow. Annoyed by its weight and significance, he nearly went to put the wallet back where he'd found it, where it would eventually be covered up, eaten up, consumed by the next storm. Then, he'd be free of it. It would stop mattering, and come spring, the wallet would be a sopping, irredeemable mess — someone else's problem. But he looked down at his watch and found that he was late. He'd promised to arrive before noon. His watch showed twenty minutes past. The wallet would have to wait. Before long, he arrived at his friend's apartment building. His hands, thrust deep into his coat pockets, felt numbed by the cold. As he ascended four flights of stairs, he became more and more aware of the wallet growing cold in his pants pocket.

"Long time no see," Clarence greeted him upon opening the door.

The two embraced in a long hug. It had been over a year since they'd last seen each other. Despite living in the same city their entire lives, neither longed to trek the three blocks to see the other with any regularity. It was only when they grew particularly lonely during the short days and long winter nights that they made any effort to meet up. They both liked it this way. Normand felt they had a close relationship, and as such, it was a relationship that didn't necessitate constant communication and effort. That's what bothered him about relationships — both platonic and romantic. The need for communication and effort in a relationship was too much complication. With Clarence, it was different. They demanded and expected very little from one another. It was what it was, and neither of them desired more. As he always did during their short visits, Clarence poured two cups of steaming black tea, and they both sat and talked of the old days when they were students.

"It's odd, isn't it?" Clarence said, setting his cup down into its saucer. "Here we are, both over thirty. Most of our old classmates left the city a long time ago, right after graduation. Yet here we are, stagnant. Sometimes I think we haven't made much of ourselves. Beyond this friendship, not much of who I was back then remains."

Normand nodded in agreement.

"I feel older than I am. I think back to when we were sixteen, picking up girls every Saturday night, drinking in secret behind the liquor store with Martin and everyone else, and I feel sad. I never thought I'd do anything great with my life, but I thought I'd do more than I have — travel, get married, maybe a couple of kids."

"I'm glad I didn't marry," Normand added. "Who needs the headache? I like my space. I wish more interesting things happened to me, but that's life, I guess. Sometimes it feels like I'm the least interesting person in this godforsaken city."

Clarence took a long drink. The conversation had dried his throat.

"Something interesting happened to me this morning. It happened on my way here to see you."

This piqued Clarence's interest, and he regarded Normand with a look of curiosity. Normand pulled the leather wallet from his pocket and set it on the table, after which Clarence unsuccessfully attempted to suppress his laughter.

"I think that's the most uninteresting thing I've ever seen. Why are you showing me your ugly old wallet? You need a new one."

He hated it when Clarence laughed at him. Always had.

"It's not mine," he said, his tone sharpening. "I found it outside the hair salon on the way here."

"Boudreau's?"

"Yea, Boudreau's."

"It probably belongs to someone inside."

Clarence shrugged, and Normand guessed that he'd grown bored with the conversation.

"No, I checked."

"Well, did you ask around to other stores? Better yet why not just bring it to the police? Whoever lost it is bound to check there first to see if anyone has returned it. Why are you carrying it around in your pocket like it's some great fortune?"

Normand didn't know how to reply. Clarence was right; the most logical course of action would be to bring it to the police. There, they could hold on to it until its owner appeared. He could rid himself of its burden and ensure that whoever had lost it would likely find it again. But something about the idea was wrong. In the amount of time that it took him to walk to Clarence's apartment, he'd grown familiar with the wallet's threatening value as though there were a link, a physical thread, tying him to it. He shook his head.

"I probably should look inside to see if I can figure out who it belongs to. I just wanted to get here on time, so I didn't think to check."

Clarence rolled his eyes and took another sip.

"Of course, ignore everything I just said except what you wanted to hear," he laughed.

"Give it over. Let's see if your interesting wallet actually holds something interesting."

Normand handed him the wallet. Clarence quickly unsnapped the thin strap that held it closed. Then, he turned it upside-down and shook its contents onto the table — two dimes, a yellowed library card, and an empty salt packet. Perplexed, Normand looked at the contents for quite some time. He'd expected more. He'd expected something necessary, something poignant, maybe even remarkable in its mundanity. But the wallet's humdrum contents sat on the table like sad relics of something that had once mattered. He reached for the library card and turned it over in his hand, careful not to further damage it. The card's edges had become soggy from the melted snow that had seeped into the wallet. The ink of its owner's name was half smeared on the front of the card, but he could just make it out — Ethel Desjardins. Clarence collected the two dimes and thrust them into his pocket.

"Don't look at me like that," he said. "It's doubtful anyone will miss two dimes. Hell, it's doubtful anyone will go looking for a wallet holding just a library card, two dimes, and a packet of salt. I know that I sure as hell wouldn't bother."

"I'll bring it to the police station regardless."

He truly meant it. Any sense of mystery had vanished with the spilling of the wallet's meagre contents, and he now thought nothing of leaving it behind at the police station. It likely wouldn't be claimed, but what interest did he have in it now? He didn't know what he'd expected to find once he opened it, but it had been something more. After another cup of tea, they listened to some old records from when they were younger. They said their goodbyes as the sun ducked behind the city, and they embraced each other one last time — knowing they'd likely not visit again until the following winter.

As Normand made his way home, he kept his eyes on the sidewalks. They were no longer white. Passing through the wet streets, car tires had splashed mud onto the pavement, turning the sidewalks brown. He fingered the wallet in his pants pocket. Disappointment lingered over him as he considered the wallet's contents. With its smeared, almost indecipherable name, the library card bothered him the most. He knew that it belonged to somebody beautiful — undoubtedly, stunningly beautiful. Such a name could not belong to anyone who was anything less than stunning. From the card, he knew three things about her (other than the undeniable fact that she must be something to look at). First, she liked to read. This fact was as evident to him as anything else. Second, she didn't carry more than two dimes, and so she was perhaps of modest means, maybe even poor. The third and final thing he knew about her was that she was important — important to him. The two had been brought together earlier in the day when he'd found her lonely brown stain of a wallet. This realization came to him all at once. Her name was reminiscent of the sweet pea ethel flowers he'd seen in a flower shop as a boy, and such a name could not belong to someone plain, someone who didn't matter, someone who could be overlooked. He pictured in her name the delicate purple blooms of his childhood — the curled petals blossoming from fragile, green stems. When he got home, he shook the cold from his body and, suddenly finding himself frightened by the wallet's gravity, threw it into his dresser drawer and tried to forget about it.

He rose early the following morning and readied himself for work as usual. Every day happened the same as the next. I thought I'd do more than I have; Clarence's words clung to him. From Monday to Friday every week, he'd work an eight-hour shift as a letter carrier. He'd done this for years without complaint. His parents, two highly educated schoolteachers, had hoped he'd follow in their footsteps. Throughout his childhood, they'd try to instill in him the importance of going to a good university and settling down with a nice woman. But this had all seemed complicated to him. He'd decided early on in life that it was not worth the effort and struggle. After receiving his diploma, he had settled into a simple life and had, up until now, never considered striving for more. His letter carrier work was often dull, but it was also comfortable and predictable. The spring and summer months were easy. The job became more difficult when the snow began to fall, and the days shortened. His toes would freeze in his inexpensive, soaked boots. Winter meant starting his route early in the morning before the sun rose and ending around dinner time when the sun had already set. Still, he rarely missed a day and was always commended for his careful and consistent work. Now he felt shaken, weakened by an unanticipated ache for more.

As the week progressed, he worked his route mechanically and without much thought. It wasn't until Thursday that he realized something unnerving — he'd developed a new habit. He also carried the wallet with the heavy mailbag filled with birthday cards and bills that he kept slung over his good shoulder. He brought it about as though he owned it, and in a way, felt he did. He was responsible for it now, and each time he delivered a letter or parcel, he looked for her name — growing increasingly impatient and dejected every time he failed to find it. By the end of that week, he'd lost all hope. He resolved to rid himself of the wallet. He'd throw it into the snow and forget about it. He'd pretend it never existed. The responsibility of it bore down on him. The intimacy he felt for this faceless name nauseated him. In a rage, he pulled the wallet from his pocket mid-route and flung it towards the nearest snowbank. But his throw had been clumsy, and instead, the wallet landed not in the snow but besides the overflowing trash cans opposite a large apartment complex.

"Good riddance. With the trash it goes," Normand mumbled into the cold.

When he'd come to the end of his route, he still felt no better for having gotten rid of it. He'd come to a disturbing realization that he'd never be able to cleanse himself of it. Whether he carried the wallet in his pocket or left it abandoned beside trashcans, it nonetheless belonged to him. As he turned towards home with an empty mailbag, he still carried a significant burden.

He sipped his soup and watched as freezing rain fell outside his window. Freezing rain meant that he might not have to complete his route. The streets would be tarred in slippery, silver ice too treacherous to travel by foot or car. He needed the break. After dinner, he tried to read the paper but did not retain any of what he read; his mind simply circled the same paragraph over and over until he tired himself out. Everything bothered him — the way his clothes felt against his skin, the sound of water trickling from the leaky faucet, the smell of newsprint. Even the temperature of his apartment kept him from sleeping. He shivered in the night, and then felt on fire with rising heat that began at his toes and travelled up his spine and into his aching head. He pictured the wallet lying amongst the trash cans, solid with freezing rain. He imagined the already smeared name on the library card growing fainter and fainter, soon to be erased from existence. Her name — her beautiful name that was to him so intimate — would be forever lost. His regret disgusted him, and he felt agitated with need. He had no choice but to go out and retrieve it. It could not wait till morning. It couldn't wait another moment. At half-past two, he sprung up, put on his warmest winter coat, and headed out into the dimly lit streets. The rain struck his face like fragmented glass, and a violent, groaning wind made the night that much less bearable. It took him almost an hour to walk the slippery sidewalks from one part of his route to another. His progress was slow, and he waddled carefully so as not to fall and hurt his already strained left shoulder. All the while, an awful, almost inconceivable thought plagued him — what if someone else had found the wallet? What if, upon walking, someone caught it out of the corner of their eye in the same way he had? A brown stain in the snow. What if they'd simply thrown it away, deeming it trash unworthy of consideration? It caused him great grief, and he knew that, if possibility were to be a reality, he might not be able to stand it.

Finally, the collection of trash cans appeared. Normand approached the area cautiously, penguin-walking his way over. A wide sheath of ice had formed on the ground, and, in the dark, it was difficult for him to maneuver. The streets were all but deserted at this time of night. The windows of the empty parked cars were opaque with ice. Silver icicles hung from streetlamps, glistening celestially in the light. He breathed for what felt like the first time in his life when he saw the brown leather frozen between a pair of trash cans. Under the glow of the streetlamp, he plucked it up and, gingerly, the way one removes a woman's dress, peeled the ice from it.

It was after three in the morning when he returned to the warmth of his apartment and pulled his coat away from his stiff and tired body. After rubbing his hands together to wake and warm them, he sat down at the kitchen table and opened the wallet. The act was an intimate one, erotic — he delicately opened its folds and retrieved the wet library card and mostly disintegrated salt packet. He uttered a throaty groan.

The name on the library card had been smeared beyond recognition. It no longer existed. Ethel Desjardin had died — the erasure of her name an erasure of her essence. Her departure from his life overwhelmed him, tortured him, set fire to him. On the verge of delirium, he excitedly poked through the wallet in search of something, anything, that would bring her back to him. That's when he saw it, and he wondered how it had gone unseen for so long — a small pocket likely meant for receipts and business cards, barely visible. It felt like prayer when he opened the pocket and pulled from it a small, folded-up photograph. She'd come back to him. There she was hair curled and half pinned at the base of a slender neck, dark eyebrows, and thin, bird-like shoulders leading down to the soft swell of her breasts. While her name had spoken to him of fragrant gardens, had brought the aroma of sweet pea ethel flowers, her face in its beautiful simplicity illustrated something different — possibility. He knew that he had to find her and that his life would only begin to matter once he did.

He did not go to work the next day. His route had not been cancelled, although the freezing rain had only ceased in the early hours of the morning. He nonetheless called out, feigning a cough. After breakfast, he set out to find Ethel. He walked the streets desperately and without direction as a colourless, eggshell sun dangled above him. He searched his mind for ideas as to where she might and eyed the picture for signs of where he might find her. The information had to be there — in this picture, in her eyes — but the library card was the only real clue he had.

The library building itself was a tall, ancient thing — brick, with a broad arched entryway, erected long before his birth. He felt confident that, within its walls, he'd find some critical piece of information that would lead him to Ethel. He hoped that the librarian had once seen her, had helped her find a book, had stamped the back of some classic novel, and had wished her a good day. He wondered what it would be like to hear her voice, smell her, and feel the gentle heat emanating from her body. Once inside, he descended the echoing hallway until he reached the check-out desk.

"What can I help you with today?"

The librarian, an elderly woman, sounded bored and barely looked up from her magazine.

"Have you seen this woman?"

He held the small photograph where she could see it.

"Her name is Ethel. Ethel Desjardins," he continued. "I found her wallet. I'm just trying to return it. She had a library card."

The librarian squinted and contorted her lips.

"No, the name doesn't ring a bell, and I'm pretty sure I haven't seen her before."

"Are you sure? I just want to return the wallet."

"Sorry. I usually remember faces and names. I'll let her know that someone found the wallet if I see her. I can take your name."

The idea of her wandering into the library and leaving with a meaningless name troubled him. His name wasn't anything special. It was a name like any other name. He wanted her to see him, to see all of him. Only then would she know how important they were to one another.

"Thank you anyway. I'll keep looking."

Normand wished her a good day and left. Outside, he looked around the street with an anguished spirit. Across from him was a dress shop, and further down the road, a café served baked goods and sandwiches. He studied her picture. She wore a simple dress. He doubted she cared much for fashion. But, books, books she liked. There was a bookstore a street away, and he knew that someone who enjoyed reading would visit libraries and bookstores. He half sprinted towards the store, carelessly splashing through cold puddles of melted ice, wetting the legs of his pants halfway up to the knee.

He found the store open, with a handful of patrons inside — a boy and his mother sitting at a table and leafing through a picture book, an elderly woman exploring one of the aisles, a teenaged girl sifting through a stack of magazines. A few other people milled about the stacks, diligently searching for something to purchase. Normand approached the cashier.

"Have you seen her?"

There were no introductions, no "good day," or small talk. The air around him had condensed into something thick and wet. It threatened to consume him, chew him up into a sloppy mess, and spit him back out. The man shook his head.

"Are you sure? Her name is Ethel Desjardins — E-T-H-E-L. You haven't heard the name or seen her?"

"No, sir. I'm sorry. I don't think I've ever seen this woman."

Something within him sunk, fell to the pit of his stomach with a thud, and broke apart. He dejectedly placed the photograph back into the wallet's hidden pocket. That was it, then. He'd never find her, never hold her, never press his lips to her soft breasts and slender neck. They'd live out their lives separately. He'd go on, forever aware of what he'd failed to find, never to be relieved from his anguish.

"Sir, Sir!" exclaimed a short, elderly woman who limped after him as he left the store.

"I heard the name Ethel. Did you say the name? Ethel Desjardins?"

"Yes! Have you seen her?"

He again pulled the photograph from the wallet. The old woman drew a sharp breath and took the picture into her hand. Her arms quivered, and the two books she held against her chest fell down onto the wet pavement. They both stood there, neither of them speaking, her books softening in a puddle.

"Do you know her?" he finally asked.

"My granddaughter," she choked. "Where did you find it?"

"Outside Boudreau's hair salon on Fraser. I found it in the snow. Do you know where she is? I'd like to return the wallet to her in person."

She inspected the photograph with tenderness. Then, she placed her hands over her face and wept.

"My granddaughter."

"Do you not know where I could find her?"

Impatient, he clenched his jaw. He simply needed to find her. He needed to hear her voice.

"I have so few pictures of her," she wiped her tears with the back of her hand. "Even now, finding this little piece of her is a blessing. She passed last week. She and I were very close, like mother and daughter."

The old woman retrieved a tissue from her pocket and dabbed at the inner corners of her eyes. "Died," he repeated.

"She was hit by a car when she came out of the salon. Since she was a girl, I always told her, Ethel, don't forget to look both ways before crossing the street. I'm sure she did, but the driver skidded out of control in the snow. They rushed her to the hospital and did all they could, but she didn't make it more than an hour. I can't tell you how lonely I've been without her."

She folded the small photograph into her purse. Normand gave her the wallet without a word, and she thanked him before collecting her wet books and disappearing again into the bookstore. He stood there for a while in the melting streets, unable to comprehend what had happened. Ethel's death, her departure from the world and subsequently his life left him with an unimaginable burden.

He refused to answer the telephone, which rang incessantly every couple of hours. He also refused to do his route and imagined himself without work, without money, left destitute. It didn't matter.

The second day, Normand peeled himself from his soiled sheets, washed his hands and face in the bathroom, covered the mirrors with a dark cloth, and mourned.

ROBIN'S NEST

A painted sky evoked promises of a warm tomorrow — pink and yellow stretched over distant hills. Thomas looked over at the vast expanse of forest, admiring the delicate beauty of a mid-July sunset. An ocean of tall, pointed pines reached out further than he could see, melting away into the sky. Thomas' father took small sips from a thermos. He was a relatively short man with sad eyes and a dark beard he'd just recently begun to grow out. At fifteen, Thomas was already taller than his father.

"What are you thinking about?"

"The sky," his father replied.

Thomas had taken to asking his father questions, however meaningless they may be. Compared to his father, he thought of himself as complex. His father had been a simple man and, as far as Thomas knew, never one for conversation. Thomas was the opposite. He often rushed from thought to thought, reading endlessly from the books his mother had collected over the years and thirsted for conversation with a man who preferred silence more often than not. It was only during these walks in the forest that he felt at peace with his father's wordlessness, at ease with himself.

"The orange parts remind me of gooseberry jam," said Thomas.

He wasn't sure why he'd said it, but he immediately regretted having done so. The words had crept upon him. He hadn't expected them, but there they were the second he'd opened his lips, rushing forth as though they had been building up inside of him for months. Thomas kicked at a small stone and sent it hurtling down the cliffside. It fell with a dull thud somewhere in the sharp silhouettes of the pine trees below. Somewhere nearby, a robin chirred only to be answered by the echoing cuck-cuck-cuck of another — a conversation between equals. But there he was, human, breathing, watching a vibrant sunset fade to grey, weighed down by shame and by guilt for even having mentioned gooseberry jam. His father left his side and sat on a large boulder, eyeing the muddy soil that coated his boots. He took another sip from his thermos and burped quietly behind closed lips. Thomas took a seat next to him and thought about his mother. He thought about the way she'd stood over the stove in the summer, closely watching a boiling pot of smashed gooseberries. It was an image that had stuck with him throughout his childhood. It was his favourite memory of her.

He remembered the blanched light and how it would filter in through the green curtains. He remembered her. He remembered with great pleasure her gentle simplicity, her sing-song voice and the way she hummed the tune to "Over the Rainbow" as she stirred the pot.

"Make sure to stir it regularly after you add the sugar," she'd told him once when he'd asked to help.

He'd usually play the role of an observer, standing beside her. While his father worked, he'd watch her in awe. He'd watch her, marvel at her the way most people stare in wonderment at stars glinting in the night sky. He'd listen to her voice the way one listens to a beautiful song. He thought of this time — her pensive, wordless tune, the sour-sweet smell of boiling gooseberries, his bare feet against cracked linoleum. Nothing had ever felt more important than those moments.

Even now, watching the sunset next to a father who might as well not be there at all, he could hear her song lingering somewhere above the tall, dry grass, mingling harmoniously with the chorus of chirping crickets. He yearned to go home to shadows painted and stretching across the old fence surrounding the yard, to his mother's lips against his forehead, to mason jars of gooseberry jam cooling on the counter. Only now, he knew that the kitchen waited, unlit and empty. The fence had fallen beneath the weight of a winter storm months ago; its pieces were strewn about like discarded bones.

"Might as well beat the dark," his father said.

Thomas saw that his father's stance was unsteady as he placed the now empty thermos into a worn brown backpack.

"What do you say we wake up early tomorrow and head back out? I think it'll be nice out again."

"How do you figure?"

"The sunset," said Thomas, pointing at remnants of slowly fading colour. "Pink and gold. It usually means a nice day ahead, right?"

His father grunted and set off down the path. Thomas followed closely behind. Night came more suddenly than they had anticipated, their journey illuminated by the light of the moon. Thomas hated the house and its darkened windows. He hated that nobody was home, no yellow lamp-light, no wood fire burning in the living room, no life to speak of.

He and his father had made these hikes a routine. As soon as school ended for the summer, they would head out on an almost daily basis. A patch of the forest began in their backyard and continued for miles, containing a labyrinth of poorly maintained trails. An army of pines and old oaks stood like soldiers waiting for battle. Thomas liked to picture the forest from above; he could see it as though he were a bird flying south. He imagined the trails as dried riverbeds snaking between the trees. When he couldn't sleep, he found comfort in tracing the forest's continuous strands behind closed eyes.

Now, Thomas looked up at the expanse of night, the icy stars lifetimes away, some already dead. He feared the walls would close in on him as soon as he entered the house, and he wished he could remain outside.

After a simple dinner of pan-fried potatoes and eggs, Thomas lay awake, tormented by thoughts of gooseberry jam. He could smell the tang — the smell of past summers, of light on moss-green curtains. The scent of his mother. He felt these memories would soon shatter, would quickly break apart like pieces of fence scattered over patchy and sun-baked soil. He whispered a greeting to the moon as though it were an old friend and didn't fall asleep until the first morning light.

A thin rain fell the next day. Thomas and his father did their best to avoid each other, each busying themselves with separate tasks, separate lives. When the summer sun finally chased the rain away, they decided to head out. Thomas knew it would be a wet, unpleasant hike, but anything would be better than attempting to dodge his father's presence. The time needed to be filled. Grief had transformed itself into a sickly sort of restlessness that both agitated and exhausted him. At fifteen, Thomas carried the total weight of his father's guilt.

"We'll head off down a different trail today, the one we passed on the way up yesterday. Might find something interesting. New places are always good to explore," his father said as they set out down the main trail.

Summers in Eastern Canada were almost as temperamental as their winters. Balmy, suffocating heat was punctuated by days of rain and angry winds. Still, even this unpredictable weather was a welcomed relief from their frigid, daunting winters when temperatures routinely fell to negative twenty, and drifting swaths of snow made it impossible to leave home for days at a time. When his mother had been alive, they'd taken advantage of summers to grow as many vegetables as could be canned for the upcoming winter months. The small garden his mother had tended with care was fertile, producing large amounts of cucumbers, carrots, onions, and beets. The forest and fields within walking distance provided an excellent opportunity for foraging, which Thomas helped his mother with. He and his mother would kneel with their knees sinking into the loamy soil. They'd pick gooseberries, blueberries, and whatever other small fruit they could find scattered about like little jewels. Then, his mother would set about preserving them in jars — pickled cucumbers and onions, gooseberry and blueberry jam.

Neither Thomas nor his father knew how to tend a garden by themselves. His father had no patience for picking berries. He could not spend hours picking through bushes. The past belonged to someone else, belonged to another Thomas — someone he did not recognize now.

The main trail went straight up into the thickest parts of the forest before forking to the right and the left. They always went right. This time, they went a left. The forest floor was thick with leaves and moss. Water seeped into his boots, irritating the skin between his toes. After a thirty-minute hike, they arrived at a small clearing between the trees where a rotten tree had fallen, its limbs broken and its trunk decomposing in the damp soil. Thomas welcomed the thin rays of sunlight that pierced through knotted branches and dangling pinecones. He and his father sat on the rotting trunk together, side by side, ignoring the fact that the seats of their pants were wet. Thomas counted patches of sheep sorrel and plucked one of the fish-shaped leaves between his fingers. He handed one to his father, and they chewed on the sour grass quietly.

"Look up there," his father said, pointing up at the branches that arched overhead.

A large oak towered above them. Thomas squinted but did not see anything worth noticing.

"Do you see it?"

"See what?"

"Up there," he repeated. "You don't see the nest?"

Thomas searched the branches, trying hard to locate the nest. Finally, he saw it. It was a small brown bird's nest perched high above the ground. A gooseberry-chested robin stood at the edge of it, her head bent down to feed the gaping mouths that cried up at her. After a while, she flew off — her chicks finally satiated and quiet. Thomas' father nudged him with his elbow.

"Have a sip," he said.

He held forth a silver thermos. Thomas took it and took a large gulp, felt fire in his throat, and coughed deeply. His father took the thermos back and swallowed a mouthful.

"I was about your age the first time I tried it, too. 'Bagosse', my father had called it. Moonshine. He'd put a jar of potatoes in his bedroom closet and wait until it was ready. It'll put hair on your chest."

Thomas looked at his feet.

"I know what you're thinking. It isn't like that. It isn't like last time. You know, sometimes it gets too loud up there," Thomas's father said while pressing his index finger to his temple. "I just need to quiet it all down. It won't be like last time."

Thomas thought about last time. He thought he'd succeeded in banishing it from memory. It returned to him on the sour scent of his father's breath. His mother's right eye — a sunken shadow. His father, clinging to her hips with his large hands, his face buried in her apron, begging for forgiveness. Her white sleeve, a spatter of blood. That evening, he'd thrown his flask into the forest and had promised never to drink again. Months later, when she'd fallen ill, his father had already begun mourning her death. He thought of her illness as his punishment. At night, Thomas could hear his father imploring her to forgive him if only for her own sake.

Thomas again took the thermos and willingly drank from it as though drinking in the past. The chicks soon began crying again overhead. Their desperate sounds filled the forest. Never far away, the mother robin returned.

“You know, robins sometimes pick at fermented berries and get drunk? It’s true. I read it somewhere even though I can’t remember where.”

The little robins continued their sharp whimpering. His father’s speech was more fluid than usual, and he spoke to Thomas freely. Thomas realized that even his own voice sounded different, as though he were talking not to his father but to a trusted friend.

“You never see the fathers,” Thomas remarked.

“Why is that?”

“It’s kind of hard to tell robins apart. This one may be male. They’re usually brighter coloured than the females, and they both take turns feeding the chicks.”

Thomas thought about his mother, who had always put seed out in the backyard for the birds. One day she had found a sky-blue egg cracked in the grass, a tiny pink fetus shrivelled inside of it. She’d never again put out seed, stating that she couldn’t bear the sight of another broken egg.

His father drank down the last of what the thermos contained and stretched his shoulders.

“We should get going.”

They both stood, staring straight ahead. The mood had changed. It had become something solid, something brutal. Thomas wiggled his toes against his wet socks.

“Should we continue the way we were going?”

“Let’s head back home,” his father said. “It’ll only start raining again.”

His father led the way as they walked. Thomas could see him occasionally pause to wipe his face with his sleeve.

“Maybe we come back tomorrow if the weather is nice,” Thomas offered.

His father grunted and shrugged his shoulders, trudging forward.

When they got home, his father stumbled to the door and Thomas, his own steps unsteady, followed. Neither felt much like eating, so they both retired to their separate rooms and retired to their respective lives. Thomas slept deeply with a thick mouth.

His father never again offered to bring Thomas along on a hike. He'd simply set off in the early hours of the morning and return in time for lunch. Thomas never asked. He felt himself less alone with his father gone. The house did not stir, and even the trees outside were static. Each morning was the same. Avoidance. Moss-green curtains drawn. Bones in the backyard. Weeks later, after Thomas had settled into this life, he felt the air change. Something about the morning was different. Wrong. His father had already set off on his hike, and Thomas waited impatiently. He was bothered by some unidentified suspicion, a persistent discomfort. Half an hour passed, and then an hour. Then three hours. By lunchtime, he still had not emerged from the forest. Considering the idea that his father had gone somewhere other than the forest, he decided to check his father's bedroom in hopes of finding something, anything that might help him figure out where his father had gone. He opened the door to find a perfectly made bed; the curtains were drawn to the side to let in the light and an empty space where his father kept his hiking boots. The room looked untouched save for the missing boots. He breathed in a musty, sweet scent. It still smelled of her. Her jar of faux pearl necklaces still sat on the bedside table. A thin film of dust had collected on the lid. Her pillow, embroidered with small orange flowers, was still next to his.

Thomas waited another hour, then pulled on his boots and headed out in the direction he thought his father had gone.

The forest was different in his father's absence. There was more sound than usual. A light wind rustled leaves. Twigs cracked beneath the steps of something unknown. An unseen bird warbled loudly. Prehistoric-looking ferns that hadn't previously been noticed now stood out on either side of the trail, their lush greenery a welcome garland. Soon the path forked, right and left. Thomas held his breath and headed left down the path.

Thomas didn't quite see it at first when he neared the decomposing tree and patch of sheep sorrel. But when he finally saw it, he couldn't see anything else. A silver thermos resting on a cushion of pine needles. Above it, a pair of old brown hiking boots. His father's face, a blue, bloated ornament, was without expression. A length of rough rope pressed into his swollen neck. Death fragmented around him in sharp shards.

He fell to the ground at his father's feet. His father's body swung like a slow pendulum. He didn't cry but merely closed his eyes and scraped his fingernails against his forearms. The stench and heavy presence of death only grew stronger.

Above him, the baby robins chirped loudly, their tiny pink heads jutting up from the nest. Thomas tried to pull his father down, grasped his thighs and used all his weight, but his father, heavy with his demise, remained a slowly ticking metronome counting the forest's heartbeat.

A SUNDAY MEETING

Sunday morning, Daniel read the morning paper and got dressed when he heard the telephone ring. He didn't answer it at first, knowing who it was on the other end. He let it ring four times before he picked up the receiver. It was Cecile. Her calls usually meant that she wanted to meet, and despite his best efforts to avoid seeing her unless it suited him, she'd stop by his apartment soon after he'd hung up the phone. He knew that today, of all days, would be the same. But it was Sunday. He preferred to spend Sundays by himself. Sunday meant he didn't have to shave. Sunday meant he could wear the same clothes he'd worn the day before. He didn't need to go into the office, run errands, or even get up off the couch if he didn't feel like it. It wasn't that he particularly enjoyed Sundays. He'd merely grown accustomed to them. They dissolved into a soupy thickness. Sunday light looked different as it draped across wooden floors and white-washed windowsills. They were inactive, stagnant days that smelled of stuffy closets.

Cecile sounded optimistic on the phone, her voice high-pitched with a playful cadence. She said she'd like to stop by, that she missed him and hoped he'd have her over for the afternoon. He responded in his usual tone of voice — low and steady. He was sick, he said, coughing and sniffing into the receiver, careful not to sound too eager to avoid her company. She offered to bring him soup or tea or otherwise come over and read to him.

"How about Tuesday instead?" he offered. "I should feel better by Tuesday. I think all I need is rest."

She hesitantly agreed.

Let her be disappointed, he thought. He didn't really care one way or another how she felt. By Tuesday, she'd forget her disappointment, and all would be well again. She was just that type of person, her moods easily changeable and her spirits easily brightened by even the most minor acts of kindness. It was the thing he liked the least about her. The truth of the matter was that Daniel was handsome. He knew this, had often been told this, and used it to his advantage. His clients trusted him to do their taxes not only because he was experienced and good at his job. They trusted him in the way people trust those who look the part, the way people trust those they deem attractive, whether they want to admit it or not. He kept himself clean, kept his dark hair slicked back, and made sure that his suits were pressed and neat. The women he slept with often told him that his brown eyes had attracted them almost instantly and that his tall stature was imposing but in the best of ways. That's why he knew that if Cecile were to ever stop seeing him, he'd recover instantly. At twenty-eight, he was still young enough to live the bachelor's life, and he knew that someone like her would be interchangeable with any other woman willing to come home with him. That's why Daniel didn't care much at all when Cecile, sensing his eagerness to end the conversation, said goodbye. He liked her well enough to see her occasionally, but that was it.

He'd only just met her a few months before. She'd never told him so, but he knew that what she really wanted was a commitment — a relationship, a promise of fidelity and a future. If she had it her way, she'd spend every minute in his apartment sipping tea and talking about uninteresting things. So, why keep her around? He'd ask himself this after her visits. The sex wasn't anything special. Conversations with her were stifled because they didn't have anything in common, and she only had herself to offer. They'd talk about their day, work, her husband, and her children for a while until the inevitable time when he'd grow bored of the conversation. He'd kiss her goodbye before she left and then find a way to forget the sound of her voice. He was attracted to her, and the long chestnut hair that hung over her shoulders down to the small of her back. Her eyes took on the glimmer of fool's gold in the sunlight, and her pale skin gave the impression of wintry tranquility. Yet, he'd been with many beautiful women. Maybe the fact that she was married interested him most of all. He'd wanted her since the moment he saw the ring on her finger.

The first time he saw her was in the park where he took his lunch breaks. He'd been sitting there a while, absentmindedly eating. A group of pigeons had congregated by the bench where he sat. Sometimes, he threw them crumbs of bread. She wore a light lemonade sundress. A matching purse hung from her thin right shoulder. She walked the winding path that journeyed through the trees and past the swing sets. At one point, she stopped and bent over to pick a single dandelion that had grown on the path's edge. Her wedding ring glimmered in the sun. He felt he could love her, at least from a distance. But when, that same night, he'd taken her to bed, he realized that she had been an illusion. Yes, she was beautiful, but she no longer retained the same quality he'd seen in the park. He clenched his jaw at the sound of her voice and thought her not all that intelligent. A shame when beauty is dampened in this way, he'd thought to himself. Their sweat-beaded bodies had laid damp atop his thin-sheeted mattress, and all he'd wanted was to be left alone.

Since that day, he'd occasionally desired her, thought of her with a mild form of affection, wondered if her husband knew how she spent her afternoons. But, once he'd climbed down from between her legs, he would inevitably count the moments until she'd leave.

He was glad that he'd avoided her visit for another day. He wasn't much in the mood for anything. Deciding that he'd merely exist until Sunday was over, he occupied his usual spot on the living room couch and attempted to not think of work. He had a pile of tax papers to make his way through on Monday, but Monday was too distant to worry about. He flipped through television channels for an hour, avoiding all commercials, for they never failed to upset him. Daniel soon grew restless and wondered briefly whether his favourite café was open on Sundays. He'd stop by every Monday and Friday for a quick coffee and sandwich after work and wondered now whether the café felt and smelled the same on Sundays. Did people, no longer weary from a day of work, still shuffle in through the front door? Was the coffee still bitter, or did the barista pay more attention to making it on Sundays? Did the sun still cast the same glow through the two large windows in the front, painting chairs and tables the colour of summer squash? Did his favourite waitress, a girl not older than eighteen with a thin figure and freckled cheeks, work on Sundays?

He had nothing better to do than sit in front of the television and only half-listen to whatever was on. Why not leave the house? Why not do something different with his Sunday? The worst-case scenario would be that his favourite waitress wasn't working, that he wouldn't see her braided yellow hair or watch her patiently and accurately take note of the substitutions he wanted for his sandwich — Swiss cheese, not cheddar, no tomatoes, extra mustard, bread not too toasted. The other waitresses would usually get it wrong, forget to write something down, fuck up in some way or another. She always got it right. She'd serve him his coffee and sandwich and smile, only occasionally making eye contact. She was shy. He liked that.

The weather was pleasant, and although the sun burnt his eyes when he first stepped out from his apartment, the warmth raised his spirits. It didn't feel like Sunday. He took off down the street and kept his head down, counting his steps. Occasionally, he'd look up at a passerby, hoping he wouldn't come across anyone he knew. The idea of conversation on a Sunday was overwhelming, unappealing. His favourite waitress never conversed with him. No, she'd simply greet him, take his order, and serve him. As social as he was at work — something his clients often remarked — he was never in the mood to keep it up by the end of the week.

He continued his walk to the café, comforted by the knowledge that most people he knew spent Sundays at home with their families. Seconds melted into minutes and became indistinct. He couldn't quite remember the walk itself but only knew that he was shaken from his thoughts by the sound of the bell above the café door as someone walked out. He heard two children bickering but couldn't tell from where it came. Outside the café, a few people sat at the tables set up on the sidewalk. They spoke loudly, their conversations mingling and incomprehensible. He could see a young couple sitting side-by-side in one of the indoor leather booths through the window. The girl held the boy's hand and planted soft kisses on his neck, oblivious to the other patrons. Daniel turned away. He thought of Cecile's lips, the colour of summer. Her hand, gold wedding band on her finger, grasping him. These thoughts annoyed him, and, as he often did when he thought of her, he cleared his throat.

Daniel stood outside the café for some time before deciding which table he'd like to sit at. He didn't feel much like sitting inside. He was surprised to see the number of people that visited the café on a Sunday. Don't they have anything better to do on a Sunday? he wondered. Don't they have a family? Cafés on a Sunday were made for souls cast down into loneliness or souls, like his, that preferred to be lonely.

A waitress saw him from inside and quickly scrambled out. Before he'd had the chance to really look around, she stood before him with a pad of paper. It wasn't his favourite.

"I was going to have my usual," he said, aware that this new waitress would have no idea what his usual was. "But I'm feeling adventurous. What do you recommend?"

"People only have good things to say about the Sunday coffee and croissant special. We have chocolate or cheese croissants today."

Her voice quavered. Daniel observed the awkward way she stood before him, occasionally shifting her weight from one leg to the other as though she couldn't wait to take his order and run away.

"I'll have that."

"Which one?"

"Chocolate."

She scribbled his order on her pad of paper and as expected, took quick steps towards the door, neither smiling nor making eye contact.

While he waited for his order to arrive, he observed the people around him. An older couple sat across from each other at the table beside him. The woman with her thick neck, silver hair, and steely eyes looked at the street while her husband, a thin bird-like man, read the Sunday paper. A gentle breeze soon picked up, providing a brief respite from the growing afternoon heat. He thought this one wasn't exceedingly awful as far as Sundays go. In fact, it was quite nice to be out and about — peaceful, even. Blanched clouds moved smoothly above him like sailboats, and soon the mouse-like waitress returned carrying a variety of small dishes. She placed a cup on the table, brimming with hot black coffee. Then, she set down a plate with what looked like a stale croissant drizzled with chocolate. Beside it, she left a little container with a dollop of jam and a pat of butter.

"Would you like sugar or cream?

She looked down at her shoes.

"Neither," he replied. "Black is fine."

He smiled at her in an attempt to make her more comfortable, but she only seemed more frightened by this gesture and quickly went away. He cut into the croissant and carefully spread a thin layer of butter on it. Just as he'd expected — stale — a day-old croissant passed off as a Sunday special before the Monday rush. With a mouthful of old pastry, he saw her. He looked at her, mouth half agape, an apparition sitting beside him. She was a young woman of around twenty-five. She had taken the table where the turkey-necked old lady and the bird-like man had been seated. His stomach danced a wild jig. He wiped a few droplets of sweat from his hairline and narrowed his eyes at the stack of books piled on the table in front of her. He attempted to read the titles.

The first book, a guide to Eastern flora and fauna, did little to interest him. The second, a thin book of poetry, made him wonder about the connection between the two. Two fashion magazines, drivel. The fourth book, open in front of her, interested him the most. She slowly studied the open page, and Daniel studied her.

She wasn't what he would call beautiful. Yet, she wasn't what he would call ugly either. She simply existed somewhere in-between. Somehow dull despite its colour, her golden hair was tied up high, and she wore a dark green sweater despite the warm weather. She was thin, her breasts barely visible beneath the bulk of her shirt. Her plain brown shoes with low heels spoke of a straightforward and grounded personality. She was the type of woman that he'd never usually notice in a crowd. Yet, here she was, possessing his full attention. He couldn't pull himself away from the unremarkable woman. Was it a sexual attraction? Maybe. Daniel could imagine sleeping with her, although he couldn't say he was all that physically attracted to her frail body. Could it be the books? He doubted it. If anything, the fashion magazines and guide to flora and fauna would have turned him off. He cared little for fashion, found it a waste of time, and flora and fauna wearied him. No, it was something else that failed to loosen its grasp. He felt an unfamiliar stirring. She had terrific fingers.

Her fingers, long and slender, appeared fragile, made of blown glass.

She turned the page of her book in one smooth, sweeping motion — a careful dance. With each movement of her fingers, he could feel his blood rising to his cheeks. Her fingers weaved carefully from page to page. Her wrists moved like music as she tucked a stray strand of hair behind her ear, causing him to almost cry out to her, to clutch her and drink her in. He knew that he wouldn't survive if she got up and left. With caution, he stood from his table and approached hers. In the past, he'd never had trouble doing these sorts of things. He wouldn't think twice about approaching a beautiful woman. How much would it take to charm her? He'd always ask himself. The answer was, usually, very little. This time felt different, and he considered tiptoeing away like the scared waitress.

"What are you reading?" he finally asked.

She looked up from the book she'd been reading. The question hung in the air between them. She held the book up so that Daniel could see the front cover. It was a Mozart biography.

"Do you play the piano, then?"

Aware of how awkwardly he was standing, fidgeting, and biting at his inner cheek, he took the chair across from her. She eyed him curiously.

"No, why?"

Her eyes were ordinary. Brown.

"Well, the book," he gestured. "And you look like someone who would play the piano."

He winced, wondering why he'd said that.

"Oh."

Daniel tugged at his earlobe.

"Well," she continued. "I don't play the piano. I do play the tuba, though. I have since I was thirteen. My parents thought I should pick up an instrument, and I chose the tuba, of all things."

He couldn't imagine her playing the tuba. He couldn't imagine those elegant fingers dancing over the valves of an instrument as clumsy as a tuba. Still, he flashed her a quick, quivering smile. She smiled back and then again pushed a strand of hair from her face, revealing the soft curve of her cheekbone. Her almond-shaped fingernails were painted a muted pink. Suddenly, overcome by the silliness of the situation, he stood from the table. She stood, too.

"I should be going," she said as she pushed her chair in.

"I'd love to hear you play sometime, even if it is the tuba."

He knew it was a lie. He hated the tuba, and he hated the idea of her playing it even more. But he needed to make her stay, if only for a few more minutes.

"I don't really play for strangers," she said.

"What if we weren't?"

"Weren't what?"

"Strangers."

She considered it.

"Maybe."

"Coffee, then. We can meet again when you aren't busy. Maybe we can talk. Then, maybe you'll know enough to play for me."

Yes, he'd certainly be up for meeting her again. He'd even be willing to meet on a Sunday if it meant being able to see her fingers bring a cup up to her lips.

"Okay," she said, ripping a corner of paper from the biography.

She took a pen from her purse and scribbled down a number.

He looked at the book before she closed it. The entire page was taken up by a black and white sketch of a piano. She handed him a scrap of paper and collected her stack of books and magazines.

"Was that a grand piano?"

"What?"

"The page you were just on. There was a sketch of a piano. Was it a grand piano?"

"No, a fortepiano," she said disinterestedly. "Mozart composed and produced all of his music on a fortepiano."

"I've never heard of it."

"Not many people have. It was pretty much the first piano, the ancestor of the modern piano."

She said this playfully as though it were a joke. Then, she smiled at him, just the corners of her lips slightly upturned. It was all it took for Daniel to know. He had to have her.

He watched her figure until he could no longer hear the click-clack of her flat brown shoes, her delicate noise swallowed up by the city streets.

He couldn't help but think about the plain woman and the piano sketch. He poured himself a cup of brandy without ice, listened to his favourite jazz record, and successfully resisted the urge to call her. He regretted not having gotten her name and wondered whether it was a name that suited her.

He recited her phone number in his mind. He'd memorized it the night before and repeated it like a poem in his dreams. When he'd dressed and made himself a simple breakfast of toast and raspberry jam, he thought again of calling her. Just pick up the phone; that's all he needed to do. He stared at the phone as though contemplating life itself. Calling her this early in the morning, barely eight o'clock, would be too desperate. He'd wait until more time had passed so that he would not seem hopeless. For now, he needed to get to work.

The phone rang its shrill siren call as soon as he opened the door to leave. He picked up the receiver, already knowing who would be on the other line.

"Daniel, could we get together after work? It's urgent."

"I'm not too sure," he said, hoping to get the conversation over with. "Can I call you when I get out? I can't be late to work."

"Sure. I'm off today, so I'll be around. I do hope you call, though. Don't forget. Like I said, it's urgent, and I think it would be better if we spoke face-to-face."

“Can’t you just tell me now? I have to get to work. I don’t want this hanging over my head all day.”

“I think we should talk in person.”

He agreed to give her a call after work. He considered that she might be pregnant. They’d always been careful, but he’d heard of these things happening even with protection. Condoms could leak. Birth control could fail. Maybe she’d forgotten to take it. She was the forgetful sort, after all. If that were the case, he’d have no choice but to make the relationship more serious. No more quiet, soupy Sundays. The woman from the café, a bitter-sweet memory. He’d be forced to forget her polished, porcelain fingers and the way her brown shoes clacked down the sidewalk — leaving it in the past like a painting stashed away in an attic.

At work, he made a series of careless mistakes. He filed papers in the wrong place, twice missed calls, and only remembered at the last minute an appointment he’d made to meet with a much-esteemed client. He shuffled out from his office when five o’clock came and dragged himself home. On the way, he passed the café. Nobody sat outside. The day had been colder than usual. A gusting wind blew, and the sky, a muted grey, was heavy with clouds. He stopped on the sidewalk and peered through the two large windows of the café. She wasn’t there. He’d hoped to see her reading the pages of some book, ignoring her drink, and letting it grow cold as she absorbed each word.

There was nothing he wanted more than to merely see her. He craved to be in her presence, even if it were behind the thick glass of the window. She needn’t look at him. In fact, he’d prefer she didn’t. He just wanted to stand there in the wind, leaves scattering around his feet. He just wanted to exist there and in her presence. It had started to rain in the time he’d been standing in front of the café, and it only picked up the further he walked. Cars drove past him, their tires splashing. He thought about Cecile and decided he might not call her. He could keep the news at bay, keep his old life, keep his soupy Sundays if only he could avoid her call.

When he got home, the first thing he did was take off his hat at the door and pick up the phone receiver. Better to get it over with, he thought. Bite the bullet. He imagined Cecile sitting by her telephone and waiting for his call, the venom of bad news on her lips. If the news was so damn important, let her make the call. He slammed the receiver down. To hell with it. If he were to call anyone, it wouldn't be her.

He kept track of the time as he made a late supper — seven and then eight o'clock. Obviously, the news wasn't as crucial as she'd said it was. He planned to call the woman from the café after he'd eaten, but by then, it was already past eight. She'd find it odd for him to be ringing her phone at this time. He imagined that she was already settled in for the night with a book, her fingers cupping a mug of tea. He hoped she was in bed alone. Tomorrow, he would call her.

Work was an impossibility, an overwhelming effort, as he put off calling the woman. She chilled him. He couldn't shake it — the piano in black and white, fingers dancing over musty pages and teacup handles. He'd pushed all thoughts of Cecile to the back of his mind. Whenever he thought, he thought of the woman. He felt close to her, undeniably tied to her in some meaningful yet mysterious way. It wasn't clear to him why. If he were to be asked, he doubted he'd be able to come up with any semblance of sane reasoning. Yet, there it was, a certainty that had crawled itself beneath his skin that past Sunday. He needed to see her. He needed to see that sketch again, the one of the piano.

He considered the city library. Surely, he'd be able to locate the biography she'd been reading. Forgetting his umbrella and hat, he hurried down the stairs. The rain didn't bother him as it hit the bare flesh of his arms. He felt as though he existed now, cool rain against goose-pimpled skin.

The inside of the library was stale and quiet. An older man, short with a shining bald head, sat behind the front counter. Daniel approached him and asked where he could find the biography section and whether they had biographies on Mozart. He hadn't the time to meander about the library attempting to find a book. The man was perplexed by the request, as though nobody in the library's history had ever requested a biography of Mozart. He led Daniel down endless rows of books until he finally pointed at two volumes — one thin book with a blue spine and one heavier hardback.

"Are those the only ones?"

"Just two," replied the librarian. "We don't get many people asking for Mozart biographies."

Daniel thanked him. He couldn't recall the size or colour of the book. First, Daniel flipped through the thin book with the blue spine but saw no sketches, just meaningless paragraphs he couldn't care to read. He liked the heft of the hardback as it sat in his hands, heavy with the weight of an entire world. He leafed through the pages carefully, more carefully than he had with the thin one. At first, the sketch surprised him as though he had not been expecting to find it. He accidentally flipped past it and then flipped back. There it was — a fortepiano delicately sketched with what looked like charcoal. It was more detailed than he'd remembered it; all sixty-six keys were expertly drawn. He had the impression that this sketch had answered some previously forgotten question that he'd carried around deep inside him. A question that he hadn't realized existed until now. As he ran the backs of his fingers against the page, he realized that the upper corner had been ripped off.

Hurriedly, he flipped to the back of the book and looked at the names written on the card. Iris Hatfield. It had to be her. He could think of no other name that would suit her — wispy petals, golden, fertile anthers caressed by the wind.

It was part of him now, this lonely book with its fortepiano and the graceful, looping letters of Iris Hatfield written on the back card. Daniel watched as the librarian stamped the back of the book and had him write his name right beneath hers. Now they were inextricably linked.

Outside, the new sun illuminated the wet pavement. The streets had been washed clean. He walked home lighter than he'd ever been, all the while clutching the book to his chest as though it might float away should he loosen his grip. He knew now that he needed to call her. It wasn't a choice.

When he got home, he held the book in his lap as he dialled her number. His heart fluttered as he dialled the last number: 4.

"We're sorry, but the number you have reached is not in service."

He dialled again, this time pressing the numbers more carefully.

"We're sorry, but the number you have reached is not in service."

In a fit, he hurled the book across the room. He felt then that he couldn't live, ought not to live. A mournful cry wrenched itself free, a cry of despair, a cry of great torment. Flesh and soul burned beyond recognition. Her fingers, her beautiful fingers grasping cups, setting loose hair strands, and turning pages. Her fingers that were to him as necessary as water, were naught but a crude sketch etched into his mind. Without them, he'd remain the way he had been — a husk. Dehydrated. Forgotten by time. Swallowed up by the city. In desperation, he retrieved the book and tore the fortepiano from its prison. He taped it up to his bedroom wall, right where he could see it, and then crawled beneath the sheets.

The phone rang incessantly. Again and again, it rang until it was all he could hear — a phantom sound that had become his essence. He could only distract himself from the tormented wailing for fleeting particles of time, stealing scraps of peace, counting the individually drawn keys of the fortepiano. Every night he watched her polished opal fingers dancing a melody over the keys. He watched them as he slept — tickling, embracing, arousing the ivory until it sang. His sweaty body lay crippled in agony, blowing rings of blue smoke while the phone crooned its admonishments.

AN HONEST DAY'S WORK

Joseph was thirty-four when he quit the job he'd held for five years, a position which, over time, he'd become well known for. The decision had come as a surprise to everyone, including himself. He hadn't planned it, only woke up one morning to find that the job held no appeal and that he wanted to do something different with what was left of his life. He didn't know what he wanted to do, but he knew that being a reference librarian wasn't it. The greatest surprise was the sudden knowledge that books no longer spoke to him in the same way they once had.

His previous infatuation with books had come to him as suddenly as his apathy. It had come to him in a dream when he was eighteen. Excoriated by the possibility of an empty future, he'd one night gone to bed drunk and had had a feverish hallucination that he believed to be a call to vocation — he had been called to write. The dream had refused to leave him. Like aggressive cancer, it rooted itself inside of him. There it grew, pulsed, and ached until he could think of nothing other than books. For weeks after, he churned out pages of prose, stacks of poetry. He wouldn't let anything distract him from his mission to provide the world with a transformative, metamorphic piece of literature. His wife, who was his girlfriend at the time, had pleaded with him to find some sort of gainful employment. He wasn't a writer, she'd told him. But he'd become convinced that, somehow, he'd polish his craft and publish. To him, this vocation symbolized freedom. It represented the turning away from a future without substance, without meaning. To create something from words was to create life. In the beginning, there was the Word, and the Word was God. Words had taken on a sacred meaning.

After a year of drafts, Joseph felt satisfied enough with his poetry collection to send it out to publishers in a tightly wrapped package. Ten rejection letters were all it took for him to burn the manuscript, bury the ashes, and spit on the grave beneath which was buried an entire world, an entire life just out of reach. Afterwards, much to Mina's relief, he studied library sciences. He found work with the nearest library, a monumental building with a wide-arched stone doorway and shelves of books that almost brushed up against the ceilings. It wasn't writing, but for five years, it had been enough.

The dizzying fervour that had accompanied his love of books had become muddied with time — like a photograph of the past. In the dream, his mother (who had passed away when he was nine) handed him a thin book with a leather cover. On the cover were incomprehensible letters etched in gold. What he could recall of it struck him as silly and inconsequential, and he could not, for the life of him, figure out why it had once meant so much.

This most recent change, this most recent certainty, had not come from a dream. Joseph was glad that it hadn't. Mina would not have stood for yet another fantasy of his. The idea had merely occurred to him as undeniable fact, a truth he could not shake. He was done with books, done with static words on a page, done with trying to find meaning in something meaningless — in the works of others.

Mina had wept for days after the sudden announcement that he'd be abandoning his work to 'find something of value.' She mourned the loss of a steady income and of stability in life. Most of all, though, she lamented the image of her husband, the person she'd come to know over the years as a voracious reader and a solid man. Joseph felt guilty at first. He couldn't stand the image of his quiet wife lying in there with the curtains drawn and mirrors covered as though having suffered death.

What came next was a series of changes that Mina wordlessly accepted. Joseph refused to show up to work. He eventually got around to sending a letter apologizing for his absence but stating that he no longer worked there. Joseph detected that Mina, too, was changing with each step towards his new life. With the move to a cheaper apartment, she gained a few wiry hairs on her chin. With his continued unemployment, she gained fifteen pounds. With his harshening tone, her hands gained a persistent tremble. And, finally, with the announcement that she needed to quit her classes and work, Mina gained her words.

Mina had been enrolled in classes at the community college where she studied music. She brought these classes with her to their new, drafty apartment. They were the only thing of value she had brought with her from her old life. Her classes were a way for her to remind herself of who she was, of who she had been before all this. The change would be temporary, he'd assured her. He didn't care what sort of work she found if it provided them enough to get by until he could figure out his next step. He'd announced the news to her over coffee in the same disinterest tone with which someone announces an upcoming doctor's appointment. She'd begun crying before he could even finish.

"Please, Joseph," she'd pleaded. "It doesn't cost much for a class here or there. They're the only thing I look forward to. The least you could do is find a small, part-time job. We could work part-time and save what we have to spare after rent and bills. It would just be until you find out what it is you want to do. With a good budget and both of us at work, we could keep living here. It's uncomfortable for me, you know that. But I'm willing to bear it if it means keeping my classes."

"You already know how to play music. You've been playing the piano since before you could add two and two. What do you need the classes for anyway?"

"That's not the point. You know it's not," Mina had exclaimed, almost dropping her cup as she thrust her hands out. "I need the classes if I'm to keep surviving here. I need some purpose other than to sleep and to worry. It's not only you who needs a purpose. You tell me all the time that you need to find your purpose, but what about me? Don't I deserve some purpose in this life? Am I less of a person now than when you first married me? With just a few more classes, I could teach music instead of working in some store. It's good money to teach."

The argument made sense to him, but he'd already come to the conversation armed with feigned compromise.

"And you can get the degree eventually. Hell, get two. Get so many they start comin' out your ears for all I care. But I can't go back now. If I go back to work now, it'll take up my time. It'll cloud my mind until I can't see the next step clearly if I can see it at all. We'll be right back where we started — a meaningless job full of meaningless books, a nice apartment, and an empty life."

She'd taken a while to reply, choosing instead to stare at him with wide eyes until they could both feel how rigid that air around them had become — like a dead tree branch ready to snap given just a little more pressure.

"What does it matter if life has meaning for you and not for me? You talk about nice things and meaning as though it isn't possible to have both. It is, Joseph. Of course, it is. Far as I'm concerned, plenty of people in this city would be more than happy with the life we had. Not many people would turn up their noses at a chance for steady, well-paying work like you had. Most people would kill for an honest day's work. We were luckier than most. Don't you see that?"

"What had we ever done that had any sort of meaning? Dinner with the neighbours? Talk of politics and gossip? Your new dresses and shoes every few months? Tell me what any of it had meaning. Plenty of things in life have meaning, and I'll be sure to stumble on one that fits me soon."

"I just don't know where on earth you got this idea in your head. All you've managed to do is sit here and cross jobs off the help-wanted section of the paper. Do you know how many people scrape by on white bread and potatoes just hoping to make something of themselves? What makes you think that you're any better? What makes you think that I want to quit my classes and go to work full time just so you can chase some invisible idea of a future? Months, Joseph. Months I've been living here with smelly carpets and a husband whose miles away in his own head. Far as I'm concerned, this is it. This is how I'll be living my life — still waiting for you to find some grand purpose that might as well not exist — until I'm nothing more than a headstone and a mound of dirt."

Joseph pressed his teeth together. He felt hatred at the sharp rise of her voice. Detest, for the red stains that spilled like cheap wine across her cheeks. Hatred, for the two deep-set wrinkles between a pair of unkempt brows. Embers of hatred danced in his throat until it felt like raw meat.

"I'll tell you how you'll be living 'till you're just a poorly marked grave that nobody bothers to maintain or leave flowers for," he exploded.

"You'll be living as a fat nag. You've gotten fat. Since we've moved, you've done nothing but eat. You think I don't notice, but I do. Sometimes, I can't even stand to look at you. You sit around in your nightclothes all day eating. At least I look for work while sitting around. When you don't eat, you sleep. Maybe we'd still have some money left in savings if you spent less on butter pastries and chocolates. Maybe then you wouldn't have to go to work. This is half your fault, far as I see it. On top of it all, as if getting so fat almost none of your clothes fit wasn't enough, all you do is talk my ears off with complaints. You think I don't hear them. Oh, you putter around and mutter them to yourself, thinking

I won't notice the quiet way you complain. The carpet smells. The door creaks. We should put oil on it. The walls are thin, and I can't sleep. The heat is out again. You fill my head with this nonsense. I can't concentrate long enough to figure out what I want to do. You suck the air from the room like cake down your fat throat. Let me alone and stop eating your worries. Things will get easier then, you'll see. If you don't like it, leave. I'll manage."

Joseph felt bad. He'd expected her to cry. He'd expected her to throw hot coffee in his face, to lunge at his throat with her plump, unpolished fingers, to scream until her voice broke. Instead, she'd simply turned away and retreated to the relative safety of their bedroom. He'd felt bad enough to purchase an old portable gas radiator for cheap, lug it two blocks from the flea market, and drag it inside.

"It'll warm you," he'd told her. "You won't have to worry yourself with the drafty windows and the way the heat knocks off every few days. You won't have to worry about your bad lungs."

Mina no longer complained of the cold beneath her breath. In fact, she no longer complained about anything. Joseph got used to the radiator's metallic grumble. Neither of them ever mentioned the fight again, although they both harboured the sting of the venomous words they'd spoken. Mina took full-time work at a shoe store and, as much as possible, did her best to leave Joseph to his thoughts.

Her stillness bothered him more than her whispered complaints. When he couldn't sleep, he'd study the lumpy frame beside him. He'd watch dawn as it tepidly caressed the stranger lying asleep beside him. He no longer knew this woman. He no longer knew this bloated, quickly ageing person who resembled a woman closer to fifty at the age of thirty-five. She was to him now a collection of unrelated parts which he desperately tried to glue together into something familiar. She was a mass of yellow hair curled over a flat pillow. She was an exposed left breast, two small nipples, a maze of blue veins. She'd been beautiful once. He'd once desired her, had once loved her. He remembered the way they'd made love almost every night for the first year of marriage and the way she smelled between her legs — hints of salt and sweat.

Now there was no want. He took no pleasure in undressing her with the lights on. He often masturbated in the bathroom to memories of his teeth peeling her underwear down her thighs, exposing her as though stripping physalis husk away from golden fruit. His journey from loving her to hating her was a difficult one to trace, but he knew it had begun, had become malignant, the morning that he awoke in search of meaning. Was his marriage genuinely dead? He couldn't come up with an answer one way or another. He entertained the thought that, once his life found meaning, he'd again be able to give substance to their marriage. For now, marriage was stagnant water.

Joseph felt a chill in the room one morning in late February. He'd forgotten to light the radiator the night before. It was cold — the type of cold that gnawed at the tender skin between his toes when he pressed his feet to the floor. He stood, rubbed his upper arms, and turned the knob on the old metal machine. The gas inched forward from the radiator and hissed a promise of warmth. He contemplated not lighting it and felt a carnal pleasure. It would be easy. Painless. The gas, with no flame to burn it away, would fill their lungs until they were nothing more than a pair of ignored obituaries in the Sunday paper. He'd heard of it happening before with portable gas radiators. People would turn the knob, forget to light the flame, and go to sleep.

"Lucky bastards," he mumbled to himself as he reluctantly struck a match.

He hoped Mina hadn't noticed that he'd forgotten to light it the night before — yet another thing on her long list of quiet resentments. If she had, she didn't mention it. She woke up, got dressed, and left the apartment. Joseph settled in for the day with a cigarette, and the help wanted section of the paper. One by one, he scanned the postings and crossed them out with a red pen. Discouraged, he closed the paper and threw it across the room. Another week of nothing. There were lots of postings, lots of businesses hiring. Yet, none of them appealed to him. For most jobs, he was overqualified. For some, underqualified. The ones he could reasonably expect to get held no appeal — desk work and the like. He needed something different. He needed something colourful and exciting, something not having to do with papers, books, and pens. Something that would allow him to find himself — to see Mina again.

Wanting to leave no stone unturned, he again picked up the paper and quickly scanned each posting he'd crossed out. When he reached the end of the list, he realized that he'd forgotten one. It was a small posting, an utterly inconspicuous listing.

Seeking gardener for indoor botanical gardens. Ten greenhouses. Experience preferred but not necessary. Please drop in during business hours if you wish to fill out an application.

The address was typed out in small print at the bottom of the listing. Joseph knew where it was. He had passed by it many times on his way to work but had never gone inside. He re-read the posting two times before it felt suitable for him. This was the one. This was the work he wanted and needed. He could imagine himself surrounded by greenery even during the lifeless winter months — fluffy ferns, fragrant roses, and all sorts of shrubs and foliage flourished in his fertile mind. This was where he'd find purpose.

He quickly dressed, wrapped a thick scarf around his neck, and headed out into the city. He hated winter. Mina loved it. It was a despicable season, cold, wet, and stinking to him. It was a long walk to the windowed greenhouses. He already felt the richness of soil caked between his fingers and the way it would feel to see it all go down the drain when he washed up after work. His toes had numbed in his boots. But all the while, he smiled at the thought of a new life.

What he'd once barely perceived on his drive to work was now an oasis. Huge, mirrored buildings filled with greenery nestled within a winter-ravaged city. He entered the main building and stopped by the ticket desk.

"How can I help you today, sir?"

A smiling brunette in her early thirties greeted him. She stood tall, almost as tall as him. He smoothed his wind tousled hair back and straightened his scarf.

"I wanted to inquire about the job, the gardening job. Who might I speak to about that?"

She rifled behind the counter and produced a clipboard and pen.

"You can fill out the application here if you'd like. You could also look around the greenhouses first. We encourage our applicants to get a feel for the environment to make sure they're interested."

Joseph nodded and told her that he'd fill out the application while he looked around. He wandered first through the fern exhibit. He softly fingered the fronds of Boston ferns, asparagus ferns, and a wide variety of ferns he did not recognize. Sometimes, he'd pause to admire the delicate, tightly spiralled fiddleheads of ferns that had yet to unfurl. He marvelled at the variety and the freshness of it all and envisioned himself in another world entirely. He'd once learned that ferns were found in fossil records as old as three-hundred and sixty million years. Ferns, like books, were historical relics. But, unlike books, they held life. Real living and breathing life.

Next was the edible plant exhibit. The smell hit him first, and he stood at the entrance in awe of the strong fragrance produced by the variety of herbs in the greenhouse — dill, rosemary, thyme, and lavender all blended in a beautiful chorus, a wafting melody of scent. He'd almost all but forgotten the clipboard he held in the crook of his arm as he cupped swollen red bell peppers in the palm of his hand, tender tomatoes, and a phallic purple eggplant hanging down from a thin green branch. He thought about plucking a few vegetables and secreting them away in his coat. The more he considered the job, the more he wanted it. It certainly wouldn't pay as much as the library, but that didn't matter.

When he reached the rose exhibit, he sat on a nearby bench and concentrated on the application. Carefully, he wrote his name, address, and phone number. He jotted down his previous job experience, but upon considering how he'd left his position at the library, he soon erased it. He completed the application to the best of his ability and hoped it would be considered seriously. He couldn't imagine what he might do if it wasn't. This was the only thing that spoke to him. These vast buildings budding with life were the only thing that excited him. They enlivened him in a way he hadn't felt in years. He saw a future worth having between the trees and shrubs and vines and flowers.

He'd been alone in the rose exhibit for some time. But as he stood, he became aware of two small voices and the creeping feeling that he'd been watched. Observed. His every move and thought had been clearly organized and catalogued. Had they been there the entire time? Had they just arrived? He couldn't be sure, but he saw them there moving amongst the rounded bushes and fist-sized roses. He saw the woman's face first. She stood tall, erect, and she held the hand of a small child. There they both stood without movement, staring in wonderment a tea-rose bush. Joseph watched them, wary. Although wide in the waist, the woman had a long face and deep-set eyes. The sockets, hollowed into her skull, gave the impression of a famished spirit.

The young child soon peeked her head above one of the shorter bushes. She looked at him. She didn't blink. Outside, snow whirled and pirouetted above the windowed greenhouse. Joseph's stomach lurched. He hated those eyes, those large brown eyes. He felt that they were somehow mocking him, ridiculing him in their own befouling manner. Her slightly upturned, pig-like nose gave the impression of a gnarled devil, a misshapen imp sent to taunt him. The woman, too, looked over at him, smiled, and dipped two fingers into the center of a blooming red rose.

She swirled her fingers inside, stroked the anthers and stamen, and then withdrew her yellow pollen coated fingers.

Alarmed, Joseph abruptly turned on his heels and headed for the exit, only once looking over his shoulder to see the woman carefully suck the pollen from her fingers. The pig-nosed little girl was nowhere to be seen. He left the finished application on the desk without saying a word and stepped back out into the city. It was already getting dark. Tepid light pooled down from streetlamps creating small yellowed puddles on the pavement. He wiped his nose with the back of his hand and tried to keep himself from shivering. He felt wrong. Sick. Imprisoned by horror that he couldn't quite explain to himself. All the while home, he felt stalked by a sinister force. He could feel them — the little girl with a contemptuous grin and an upturned nose, a gaunt woman working her tongue over pollen-coated fingers. He thought they were somewhere nearby, possibly ducked behind a parked car or hidden in the darkness of a narrow alley.

When he reached the safety of his apartment, he drew the curtains shut and turned off the lights. Mina arrived from work soon after. They looked at each other. He wanted to throw himself at her feet, prostrate himself as though at the base of a holy shrine, utter prayers of forgiveness. But he merely looked at her, neither speaking nor moving. They stood that way for a while, two statues at a distance, two immovable stones. She waited, sensing that he had something to say. Joseph could feel on his cheeks that he'd been crying, but for how long, he did not know.

They both went to bed at the same time that night, neither speaking to the other. It was a cold night, much colder than he'd anticipated. He thought of tapping Mina's shoulder, undressing her the way he'd used to, learning to love her the way he once had. But he knew it would all be meaningless. It all was. Feeling the chill within himself, he stood to light the radiator. He glanced out the window and saw two shadows across the street — the tall one holding the shorter one's hand.

Joseph turned the knob on the radiator, listened for the familiar hiss of gas, and breathed.

a very good man

Eugene's father had owned the butchery for twenty years. As far as Eugene was concerned, it was twenty years wasted. He had worked in it alongside his father until he finished school and quit to start a life of his own. Selling meat in a seedy storefront was not his idea of a future. But now, ten years later, he felt that his life still hadn't begun. He hadn't figured out what it was he wanted to do, and on his twenty-eighth birthday, he finally decided that his future wasn't much of a future at all.

He'd managed to accomplish a few things, but he doubted that his accomplishments were at all impressive. At least, they weren't to his father. He rented his own two-bedroom apartment down the street from his father's place, owned a grumbling old Buick, and had kept the same job as a door-to-door salesman for a home cleaning products company since graduation. He had never been to college. His father had hated the idea of his only son being a door-to-door salesman.

"Why don't you go off to school? Better yet, stay to work for me for a while until you find out what it is you want to do. It'll pay more than a commission," he had said when Eugene first announced he was quitting to work as a salesman.

But Eugene would have none of it. His father had a small, sad life. If anything, working on commission would be a step above what his father had accomplished. It would mean working independently without someone watching over him. It would mean making money not based on time worked but on the quality of the work itself. And so, he took the job and, over the years, was successful at it. He was often lauded for his friendly demeanour, his pressure-less sales tactics, and his ability to sell more products than any other salesman at the company. Sometimes, he thought about a house, a wife, and children. Every time he seriously considered it, though, he would realize that the simpler his life was, the better. He intended to keep it that way. He'd watched his father struggle through a failing business and a failing marriage long enough to know better.

Although the butchery had at first become a staple in the neighbourhood, it was now floundering. It had happened slowly, a winding down of what had been a steady business. They'd for years enjoyed the sort of stability, but when his father lowered prices to make the meat more affordable for poorer customers, it all began to change. Soon he started extending credit to those who couldn't afford to pay upfront. He lost money, and despite its loyal customer base, the business faltered until his father could barely keep up with the bills.

Eugene tried his best to avoid his father and steer clear of his failures. He considered his father to be simple-minded both in business and in life. He hadn't heard from his father in weeks until, one morning at four a.m. he received a phone call from him.

"Eugene," his father exclaimed. "You need to take me to the hospital. Come and pick me up."

"Dad? What's wrong?"

Eugene had been washing his face and getting ready for work when the phone rang.

“I’ve lost a kidney.”

“What do you mean, you’ve lost a kidney?

He listened intently. So far, nothing about the conversation made sense to him.

“I mean what I say. I’ve lost a kidney. I went to bed last night with two, and now there’s just one. It’s gone. Can you take me to the hospital or not?”

He had no idea what to make of this. Indeed, it would be impossible for someone to lose a kidney overnight as though it were a set of car keys. Vital organs don’t just up and vanish, he told his father over the phone. He pictured his father’s kidney lodged between the couch cushions, misplaced in the junk drawer, or dropped on the sidewalk somewhere for a child to find. It was a ridiculous situation, but he decided to humour him. Eugene called into work and told his manager that there was a family emergency, then he reluctantly drove to the hospital.

The doctors took his father in straight away, assuming he was experiencing pain from a kidney stone. They carefully palpated his lower back, causing him to shout obscenities and swat at the doctors. Because his lower back was obviously tender, they ran x-rays and took his blood. Eugene waited in the examination room and listened to his father insist that the cause of the pain was the missing kidney. It had been ripped from him in the night. The doctors were perplexed. There was no wound, no redness. The blood work came back clean, and the x-ray showed two healthy-looking kidneys right where they should be, exactly where they had always been. Nothing was amiss, as far as they could tell. His father was shown the evidence, yet he persevered in his assertion that the organ was missing.

“The x-rays have been falsified,” he exclaimed from the hospital bed. “You’ve falsified them! Why? I don’t know. You tell me.”

Later that day, the hospital psychiatrist informed Eugene that his father was suffering a temporary delusion brought on by stress and dehydration. Because he didn't seem to be a danger to himself or others, they discharged him in Eugene's care with strict instructions. Eugene was to watch his father. He was to make sure that he got enough rest and drank enough water until the delusion passed. The doctors turned their attention from his body to his mind. They prescribed a barbiturate, hoping it would calm him and speed up his recovery.

Eugene moved into his father's apartment that day. It was to be a temporary move. He had to remind himself that it was not permanent, and he repeated it to himself like a mantra, unable to stand the idea of caring for this crazy old man. He wasn't sure why he felt he owed it to his father — a man who had always stood at a distance. But he knew that the butchery wouldn't survive a temporary closure. He also knew that his father was in no condition to work and that, should the butchery fail, he would have no source of income and would likely become dependent. This was something Eugene couldn't stand for — caring for his father permanently, supporting him monetarily, listening to him shuffle about the apartment in slippers and clear the phlegm from his throat. He needed to make sure that the business stayed afloat for now. Reluctantly, he called work to tell them that he'd need to take a temporary leave of absence due to a family emergency. Eugene decided that he would try to revive the business, and he hoped that the delusion would pass sooner rather than later. Only then would Eugene be able to return to his life.

He began making changes the first day at the butchery. He flipped the sign on the front door to 'OPEN,' wrote "no credit" on a piece of paper and taped the sign up by the cash register. Then, he waited for customers. Hours went by without a single one, during which time Eugene took it upon himself to slightly raise the cost of most of the meats. He reasoned that new clientele willing to pay higher prices would make up for whatever customers he lost.

Someone finally came in around noon — a middle-aged man with a balding head. He picked up a pack of sirloin, eyed the price tag, and then set it back down.

“The price of the sirloin has changed? I’ve been buying it same price here for years. Lowest price in the city,” the man said.

“Sorry. We’re under new management. Things cost more money now too. You should know this. Everything has been costing more.

“No credit either?” the man said, pointing to the sign.

“No credit. Only cash up front.”

The man sniffed, pretended to look at the canned goods for a bit, and then left.

There were no more customers. Eugene closed the store at five and marched tiredly upstairs to his father’s apartment. He expected to find that he had rested and had improved a bit, but when he opened the door, he found his father clutching his lower back, lamenting the loss of his kidney. He had crumpled to the floor and said that the pain was unbearable. His face was contorted into an awful grimace, and the veins on his sweat-drenched forehead were pulsating. He begged Eugene to bring him back to the hospital.

“There’s nothing wrong with you, Dad. Doctors said so themselves. All you need is rest and fluids. No sense in a trip to the hospital for something that’s all in your head.”

Not knowing what else to do, he sat at his father’s side with a dishtowel and patted his brow dry, trying to ignore the way his father thrashed in anguish like a dying fish. After an hour of what he considered to be mere theatrics, the pain subsided, and his father lay on the floor panting until Eugene took him to bed.

The next day, his father seemed alright. He continued to complain that he had yet to locate the kidney, but he looked well enough to be left alone. As far as Eugene was concerned, the remedy for the delusion would be to revive the butchery. If this had all started because of stress, his first order of business should be to alleviate the source of said stress.

That day, as he ordered more meat, he also ordered a selection of fish — salmon, freshwater trout, and herring. It was a small change, but he reasoned that it was a necessary turning point. More variety meant more customers. Later that night, he told his father about the fish and used firm voice to stave off any arguments. But his father had none to offer. He was not bothered by the news. He was not happy, either. He was a potted plant that occasionally needed to be watered or moved into the sun. Eugene didn't have the heart to dispose of a potted plant, although it took up too much room and had begun to turn yellow.

It wasn't until a couple more weeks had passed that Eugene began to see new faces in the butchery. Most of the old customers had stopped coming. It was just a few people at first, and then a few more. They didn't complain about the prices. A few of them commented that they were fair prices, still lower than other butcheries in the city. They also did not ask for credit, and they paid upfront. Eugene also called the old customers who owed money and asked them to pay off their debt. Only two out of fifteen did. He thought it best to write off the rest. There was no point in chasing them down.

He enjoyed the new customers that came in. Their clothes were neat and clean compared to the old clothes the previous customers had worn. The ladies came in with their hair and makeup done. Some of them smiled and flirted, much to his surprise. He was satisfied that the butchery had begun to turn a profit under his management, and he felt successful in a way he never had while selling cleaning products door-to-door. Yet, he still didn't intend to stay. No, this was his father's business, his father's future. It didn't belong to him.

"The butchery is turning a profit. We'll be out of the red soon," Eugene said that night over dinner.

He showed his father the books but knew that he wouldn't understand.

"Profit," his father repeated.

"Yea, profit."

"Mrs. Piszcesk. How is Mrs. Piszcezk?"

"How should I know? I haven't seen her."

"Not at all?"

"No."

Eugene cut his father's potatoes into smaller bites.

"Maybe she's seen my kidney. Could you ask her for me?"

"I already told you that I haven't seen her."

"Haven't seen her," he repeated in a disinterested tone. "What about you? Have you seen it anywhere? It'll go bad if we don't find it soon. Have you checked on Union Street?"

"Why on earth would I check on Union Street? It's clear across the city. Takes forever to get there even if there's no traffic. You have two perfectly good kidneys, Dad. Doctors said so themselves. Could you please eat before it gets cold?"

"Doctors said so themselves," he said in a mocking tone.

That night Eugene lay awake on his father's lumpy couch, thinking up ways to end his delusion. He considered placing him in the psychiatric hospital but ultimately decided against it. He felt little for his father, but he worried that people in the neighbourhood would think him a bad son should he go through with it. It would be his last resort. The only other option he could think of was to simply take over the business permanently. If he made enough, he could hire someone to care for his father. Why not? He had already started making a success of it, after all. With time, it would become his — something he'd built from the ground up. It would become his own. If his father stayed crazy, perhaps it wouldn't be so bad to keep the business running.

His father slept in the next day while Eugene opened early. Two people were already waiting at the entrance. One was a well-dressed young man holding a newspaper beneath his arm. He seemed to be in a hurry, tapping his foot impatiently while Eugene unlocked the door. The other was a crooked woman with a hump on her back. She stood far behind the young man and blew her nose into a tissue which she then frowned at and stuffed into her coat pocket. Eugene let them in.

The young man headed straight for the selection of fish. He picked up two packages of salmon, one in each hand, and inspected them from all angles. Then, settling on the one he found the most appealing, he approached the cash register.

"That'll be all today?" Eugene said, smiling, as he rang up the purchase.

The man nodded as Eugene wrapped the package in brown paper. Then, he printed the receipt and handed it to the man, who quickly exited without a word. The day had already started off on the wrong foot.

The hunched woman still stood by the door. She looked at Eugene, frowning.

"You're not Alfred," she finally said.

She approached the cash register.

"No, I'm afraid not."

"Where's Alfred?"

She stank of onions.

"He's not here. I'm his son, Eugene."

Upon hearing this, the woman's demeanour changed. She smiled at him. Eugene noticed that her lipstick was sloppy — smeared a bit at the corner of her mouth. He guessed that she was at least seventy-five. He smiled back at her, encouraged to see a friendly face.

"Well then, it's nice to meet you. Where is your father?"

"He's sick right now, so I'm managing the business until he feels better."

"Sick? Oh, dear. I hope it's not serious. Always such a nice man, your father. You know, he was the only butcher in the city that let me buy on credit. I always paid him back, too. A good man. A very good man. What's wrong with him?"

"It's nothing really. He should be back on his feet soon. He needed a rest, is all."

The woman nodded.

"Do tell him I said hello, and that I hope he feels better soon."

"What's your name? I'll be sure to tell him."

"Maureen," she said. "Maureen Piszczezk. He'll remember me."

Eugene thought about what his father had asked him. For a second, he considered asking her whether she knew anything about a kidney. Then, remembering that the whole thing was a delusion, decided against it. *I'm becoming just as crazy as he is*, he thought.

"Can I help you find anything today, Mrs. Piszczezk?"

"I'll just get my usual."

She hobbled over to the meats on a bad leg and selected a small package of ground beef and a packet of chicken gizzards. Eugene rang up her purchase.

"One pound of ground beef and a package of gizzards. It comes out to one-dollar and fifty cents."

"One dollar? Prices have gone up, have they?"

Eugene nodded, and the old woman sighed, looking into her coin purse.

"I don't have enough on me. Could you put it on credit?"

He pointed at the sign taped to the register.

"Your father always let me take things on credit. I always paid him back, too."

Eugene flipped through his father's old notebook and located her name. Her account was paid, and it was true that she had regularly come in to make payments. He closed the book. If he extended credit to one, he'd have to do it for everyone once word got out.

"Sorry. Things have changed, and we no longer give credit."

She looked sadly at the two packages of meat. Her lips trembled.

"Are you sure? I can't afford to buy meat anywhere else. Your father always had the best prices. The beef was supposed to be for tonight's supper. My son, he's coming to visit for the first time in a year. I want to make him something he'll like, but we don't have much at home."

Eugene stared blankly at the woman, holding his ground, until she left. Later, he checked the dates on all the meats and found that the package of chicken gizzards was expired, as was the ground beef. He threw it all into the dumpster on his way out.

He closed early and decided to take a walk. It was a drizzly night. Papier-mâché moonbeams drenched the city in opaque light. Eugene walked far from the street where the butchery was — the street where both he and his father had lived their entire lives. He walked until he came to a road with well-maintained brownstones.

A few cookie-cutter trees lined the sidewalk, and Eugene carefully stepped on the fallen leaves, listening for the crunch. He thought about how well-maintained the brownstones were, how well-manicured the trees looked. When he came upon a convenience store, he purchased a pack of cigarettes. He hadn't smoked in years but felt that the occasion merited a smoke. He couldn't figure out why he felt so downtrodden. Was it the woman with her sad eyes? Was it his father's condition? He doubted it. His father's condition did weigh heavily on him at times, but his worry was less about his father and more about his own future. How would things turn out? Would he take on the butchery as his own? Would his father recover and take it out of his hands? If so, would his father maintain the he had made, or would he revert to making poor business decisions? The future, as it always was for Eugene, was too abstract to put together.

He'd smoked two cigarettes before he decided to turn towards home. All the while he admired the gossamer stars draped against the night sky. He planned to fix his father some supper as soon as he arrived. Maybe he would tell him, as gently as possible, that he'd take care of the business for as long as needed.

As he approached the building, he took a right into the alley beside the butchery to smoke one last cigarette and found his father digging through the dumpster. It was a large, blue dumpster where Eugene tossed scraps of meat — unusable bits and the occasional piece of expired steak. He didn't turn around when Eugene called to him. Instead, he continued digging elbow deep in the dumpster as though he had dropped something inside of it.

"What the hell are you doing?"

Eugene seized his father by the shoulders and spun him around. Looking into his panicked eyes, he suddenly and without explanation clasped him to his chest. Eugene wondered why he hadn't noticed how much taller he was compared to his father. His father's head rested on his shoulder. He did not fight back but merely remained there, nestled in his son's arms.

"What the hell are you doing?" Eugene repeated.

"I found it."

He wrenched himself from Eugene's arms and presented a wet fist — spreading his fingers open to reveal what he'd found. At his feet was a ripped-open package of expired chicken gizzards. His father held in his hand a palm-full of tiny, raw organs.

"My kidney!"

He shook his wet hand.

"Why'd you throw away my kidney? Why'd you chop it all up?"

Eugene looked at his father — a shrunken, deranged old man holding a handful of bloody gizzards.

"You stare at me so stupidly as if you don't know what I'm talking about. You tossed it away with the bad meat."

His father threw the expired gizzards back into the dumpster and wiped his bloody hand on his pant leg.

"Useless now! It's all useless. What good am I to this world?"

Eugene lunged at him; arms outstretched. He tried to again take his father into his arms. He felt he needed to. He needed to hold him, beg his forgiveness, plead for understanding. He needed to tell him that he was sorry, and that he would be a better son — a better man, a good man. But his father pushed him aside and ran to the apartment.

He locked the door, leaving Eugene to sleep in the back room of the butchery. At dawn, Eugene unlocked the door and took the "no credit" sign down from the register.

Photo (2023) courtesy of the author.

ABOUT THE AUTHOR. *Angel T. Dionne is associate professor of English literature at the University of Moncton Edmundston campus. She holds a PhD in creative writing from the University of Pretoria, and is a founder and head editor of* Vroom *magazine. Her writing has been featured in journals and anthologies including* Surrealists & Outsiders, Everyday Fiction, The Molotov Cocktail, Crack the Spine, Chicken Soup for the Soul, Crab Fat Magazine, Apocrypha & Abstractions, Petrichor, Indefinite Space, Writers Resist, Sortes, SurVision, *the Lucy Writers' Project, and* JAKE. *She lives with her wife and their cats. Readers can find her on Instagram.com @angel.t.dio_ and on Weebly @angeldionne4.* Sardines *is her debut short fiction collection.*

www.ingramcontent.com/pod-product-compliance
Lightning Source LLC
Chambersburg PA
CBHW031307120726
47906CB00003B/928

* 9 7 8 0 9 9 1 6 2 2 2 5 2 *